LONG SHOT

David didn't believe that "The X-Files" stood a chance of being picked up.

The way he looked at it, shooting the pilot would give him some satisfaction, a month in Vancouver, British Columbia (where the show was to be filmed), and a paycheck. That would be the end of it. "The X-Files" would never be heard of again, and he'd move on to his next film a little more experienced, and with a little more money in his bank account.

But first, he had to land the part . . .

THE X-FACTOR:
DAVID DUCHOVNY

Other Avon Books by
Chris Nickson

Go, Ricki!

THE X-FACTOR

THE UNAUTHORIZED BIOGRAPHY OF
X-FILES SUPERSTAR
DAVID
DUCHOVNY

CHRIS NICKSON

AVON BOOKS ▲ NEW YORK

THE X-FACTOR: DAVID DUCHOVNY is an original publication of Avon Books. This work has never before appeared in book form.

AVON BOOKS
A division of
The Hearst Corporation
1350 Avenue of the Americas
New York, New York 10019

Copyright © 1996 by Chris Nickson
Cover art by Swanell/CP/Retna Ltd.
Published by arrangement with the author
Library of Congress Catalog Card Number: 96-96459
ISBN: 0-380-78851-9

First Avon Books Printing: December 1996

AVON TRADEMARK REG. U.S. PAT. OFF. AND IN OTHER COUNTRIES, MARCA REGISTRADA, HECHO EN U.S.A.

Printed in the U.S.A.

RA 10 9 8 7 6 5 4 3 2 1

To the memory of Carol Schutzbank, 1961–1995,
the X-Phile and good friend
whose spirit was too big for two hearts.
You are missed.

Contents

Introduction
Click On Icon to
Open File

It used to be that no one would ever have considered an FBI agent to be a sex symbol. Efrem Zimbalist, Jr. was about as close to an Agency pinup as you ever came. Until fall 1993, that is, when we were all introduced to Special Agent Fox Mulder.

Startlingly handsome, well groomed, he seemed every inch the perfect FBI agent. And with an impressive academic background, he'd won fame at the Academy in Quantico for his psychological profiling of serial killers. He looked like the type who'd be set on the fast track to promotion.

Except there was a deeper side to Mulder. His obsession with the X-Files, those strange cases that defied rational explanation. Mulder took them on, and began learning things. Dangerous things . . .

Of course, in reality there is no Special Agent Fox Mulder. And as far as we know, the FBI doesn't keep a room full of X-Files. But for millions of people every week, in more than sixty countries and languages, Mulder, Scully, and the X-Files exist.

More to the point, David Duchovny exists. That's something to please X-Philes and members of the David Duchovny Estrogen Brigade (his unofficial fan club) all over the globe. To them, and to everyone else who tunes in the show religiously, week in and week out, he *is* Fox Mulder.

Every episode generates frantic messages across the Internet, comments about his lines, his looks, his humor, and his clothes. When he appeared in tiny red Speedo swim trunks, computer screens all over America lit up with fantasies.

That's the power he's been able to bring to the role.

And, in return, it's made him a celebrity.

It's ironic, then, that he almost turned the part down.

When he was offered the chance to play Fox Mulder, David wasn't convinced. He had a previous film commitment, his movie career was finally starting to take off, and he didn't truly believe that "The X-Files" stood a chance of becoming a hit show; less than that, really.

He didn't even think it would last a single season on the air.

But it has, and it's gone on to prove him wrong by finding a mass audience internationally, and letting him make his biggest mark yet.

There's a lot of David Duchovny in Fox Mulder. Both are extreme intellects (Mulder studied at Oxford, Duchovny at Princeton before going on to do graduate work at Yale). Both are handsome and hunky—six feet tall, one hundred and seventy pounds, wearing a forty long suit and size eleven and a half shoes. Both are active—Mulder is a jogger, David plays basketball and studies yoga. They both write—David pens poetry, while Mulder (under a pseudonym) contributes to *Omni*. And each possesses a very dry wit. In Mulder's case, the humorous side of his personality is slowly being explored on the show. With David, it's there in slightly self-deprecating form in every interview he gives.

But there's also a great number of differences. Don't imagine for a minute that when you see Fox Mulder on your television screen you're also getting the real, total David Duchovny.

Mulder is a true New England WASP. Duchovny is a more interesting ethnic mix, with a Russian Jewish father and a Scottish mother, raised in the racial melting pot of New York's Lower East Side. Any advantages he

gained weren't handed to him; he grabbed
them with his mental and physical prowess.
And, unlike Mulder, his sister was never abducted by aliens when he was a boy.

Perhaps no one is more surprised than David
himself that he's become a star. As it was, even
becoming an actor wasn't something he'd considered until he was in his mid-twenties. He'd
always imagined he'd have a career as an
academic, specializing in literature. The jump
from one to the other couldn't have been
farther or more more profound. But in a short
time, David had results when he was cast in a
Lowenbrau television ad.

At that point he lost interest in academia,
abandoning his PhD thesis (the only degree
requirement he still had to fulfill to gain his
doctorate), and plunging into acting full-time.

From a role in a small independent film,
Henry Jaglom's *New Year's Day*, he slowly
moved up the scale, with featured roles in *Julia
has Two Lovers*, *The Rapture*, *Venice/Venice*, *Chaplin*, *Beethoven*, and *Ruby*. But although he was
working regularly, they weren't the kind of
parts that would ever get him noticed.

That didn't happen until *Kalifornia* came
along in 1993. As the second male lead (and
the hero this time) behind Brad Pitt, David was
very noticeable and very strong, playing a
yuppie writer making a tour of murder sites.
Whether it would have been his break-

through, we'll never know. But it certainly helped in obtaining the role of Fox Mulder. While not a huge hit, *Kalifornia* made an impact because of its tough and violent story.

By then David was already working in television, first portraying the transvestite DEA agent in David Lynch's bizarre "Twin Peaks," then as the cuckolded narrator for the "Red Shoe Diaries," soft-core pornography on cable. After starring in the pilot, his appearances were brief, a minute at the beginning, another at the end of each episode, but again, it earned him money and exposure.

The real breakthrough was "The X-Files."

The show has changed his life in so many ways. These days people definitely know who David Duchovny is. They want his autograph, want to have their picture taken standing next to him. There's a constant stream of reporters eager to interview him. And, of course, he's become the thinking woman's sex symbol.

That's the upside, the plus. But "The X-Files" has also made him into a man without a home, or even a life to call his own. For ten months out of every year, he lives in a sublet apartment in Vancouver, Canada, where the show is filmed, working twelve to sixteen hours a day, five days a week.

When the weekend arrives, he either flies down to Los Angeles to see his girlfriend, actress Perrey Reeves, or she comes to see him.

Although he can well afford it these days, David doesn't have a real home in southern California, just another series of sublets he can use between shooting seasons.

And that's a situation that doesn't look as if it'll change anytime soon. As long as the show remains popular (and its popularity continues to climb, as more and more people become hooked on its unusal premises), David will be spending most of his year in British Columbia, with only his dog Blue (named for a Bob Dylan song) for company most of the time.

That's the price he pays for his fame. But that's just as well to him. As he says, "Most of my life takes place on the inside. Nothing much sticks to me."

As Mulder, David has a tough acting job, keeping the passion simmering under a very deadpan surface.

"If I'm to take any pride in what I do on the show, it would be in bringing what some call my understated style to TV, which is not an understated medium."

In that he succeeds perfectly.

There's nothing over the top in his portrayal of Mulder. Like an iceberg, seven-eighths of the character is hidden beneath the surface, held in reserve. Only when the waves churn does the audience get a brief glimpse of what's down there.

And that's part of what makes David so

appealing as Mulder. Like the thoughtful man he really is, he keeps his cards close to his chest, playing them smartly and sparingly.

In many ways he's redefined the role of the intellectual on prime time television, which usually has no room for brainy people. Unlike the beautiful and the evil—preferably malicious, soap opera evil—brains and popularity aren't regularly associated on TV. But he's proved it's perfectly possible to be bright and still have plenty of fans, to be a hero (or quite possibly an anti-hero) with a mind as well as looks and a great body.

There's a spareness to his acting. It's lean and honed-down, which helps make the character so believable. Mulder might be disparagingly nicknamed Spooky, but there's nothing weird about the style David brings to the part. He's as straight down the line as any Joe Friday.

Of course, what we see on our screens is David now, thirty-five years into his life. In that time he's undergone any number of changes, not only of career, but also of personality. He's learned a lot about himself, the things that make him tick. He's learned what things work for him and what don't.

One of the things he has a chance to do these days is more writing. He's worked on a couple of episodes of "The X-Files," and will likely work on several more. He's also a poet who's been known to read his work at open mikes in coffeehouses. Wherever you scratch him, the intellectual isn't far beneath the surface. David is a man who constantly thinks about what he's doing, considers and evaluates it, weighing the possibilities.

Perhaps the greatest irony is that someone like that should have become so popular in television, a medium which has tended—especially in recent years—to laud mediocrity and aim for the lowest common denominator in an attempt to lure audiences. That's made David stand head and shoulders above the pack, in a way that might not happen so much in the theater, or even in movies.

But it's hard not to smile at success. David may not have believed that "The X-Files" would make it, but now that it has, he's not about to walk away from it. And who can blame him? The work might be hard, but the results are more than gratifying.

Even so, he can see an end to all this sometime in the future, a day when he'll say goodbye to Mulder.

"I'd like to see Mulder die one day," he said in *Shift*. "Not soon, but one day he should die." Then he added, "He should get laid, and then die."

To many that's an unspeakable thought. But not to David. The future will always be there, beckoning with new challenges. And they've become something to look forward to, not to be afraid of. For now, "The X-Files" is big business. It plays all over the world, fans regularly attend conventions, and sales of books associated with the series boom, as do sales of tee shirts, mugs, and all kinds of of paraphenalia. Still, like any series, its time will come and go. Mulder may not die. He may just be quietly cancelled at the end of a season, the result of an executives' conference (and, given the paranoia inherent in the series, that might be more appropriate). However it happens, his time is finite.

But David will be around long after Mulder's disappeared. He's made his mark, he's known now, a bankable quantity with millions of fans in many countries.

That's all for the future, though. At the moment "The X-Files" continues to soar in popularity, as does David. But how did he reach this point? What is it about him that attracts people, especially women? Who, really, behind that suited exterior, is David Duchovny? And what exactly *does* make him tick?

ONE

Scroll Back to Childhood

Amram Duchovny was born in Brooklyn, New York. His parents, Russian Jews, had emigrated to America, and he was the first of their children to be born on U.S. soil, really free in a way he could never have been in his parents' land. He never returned to his homeland, but the large enclave of Russians who lived around Brighton Beach in the borough gave a warm feeling of the way things could have been. Russian, in all its dialects, was the common language, rather than English. The smell of borscht and beets filled the restaurants and spilled out onto the sidewalks. Samovars full of tea steamed in peoples' homes.

Conversations about the Communists who were in power in Moscow, about literature, about religion, lasted long into the night. It was an exhilarating place for a young boy to hear these endless exchanges of ideas.

But Amram's sights were set beyond the small horizons of Brooklyn. His heart might be Russian, his soul Jewish, but he was an American, born and bred. And that was important to him. He was determined to make something of himself in this new land. English became his main language. In school, his education touched on things that his parents had never been taught, new ideas, new politics, new ambitions. Unlike Russia, even the Russia of the old men who gathered and talked for hours, America was a free country, a place where a man could do and be whatever he wanted. That was the lesson underlying everything, and Amram listened well.

As he grew, becoming more American was important to him. He dropped the "h" from his last name, making it Ducovny, in an attempt to Americanize it.

The one thing that he didn't try to change was the fact that he was Jewish. Unlike Russia, in America he had the freedom of religion; there were no pogroms here. All around him were so many other Jews. Many of the Hassidim, obvious in their hats, ringlets of hair hanging down their cheeks, and beards, who made their livings in Manhattan's diamond district, lived in Brooklyn. The synagogues were full on Fridays and on all the High Holidays. It was common to hear Hebrew and Yiddish on the streets—they could almost have been the third or fourth languages of the area.

Amram realized that being Jewish was, in a way, more important than being Russian. The religion transcended national boundaries, setting a whole group apart. The Jews were, from their history, God's Chosen People.

At the same time, this *was* America, in the twentieth century, a land where progress was king, and Amram saw no need for his religion to keep him locked in the past. A Jew could play a full role in the modern world. So that was the way he kept Judaism in his own life.

As he grew, Amram began to show real talent as a writer. He could put words together smoothly, create characters, tell stories on the page. And he loved doing it. But to make a living as a writer was tricky; there was never any certainty to it. Who knew when, or how much, you'd get paid. It was honorable work, but a man needed an income.

So, after graduation from high school, Amram Ducovny became a publicist for the American Jewish Committee. As much as anything could be, it was the perfect job for him, involving both Judaism and writing. Above all, it brought in a paycheck every week.

To make his life easier, rather than commuting from Brooklyn into Manhattan every day, Amram moved into New York, to the Lower

East Side. In the 1950s this was still a very Jewish area, as it had been for the better part of one hundred years. For a long time it had almost been a Jewish ghetto, the place where immigrants came after landing at Ellis Island, to live with relatives, work in the sweatshops that had sprung up all over the area, to save their money and move on to better lives.

But slowly the Lower East Side was beginning to change. While there were still more yarmulkes than bare heads on the streets, a few bohemiams were starting to move in, attracted by rents that were lower than in Greenwich Village.

It was here that Amram met his wife-to-be, Margaret, known to everyone as Meg.

Meg was born and raised in Scotland, before her parents moved to New York. She was still young, a teenager in high school, when they fell in love. In fact, she barely had her diploma when they married and set up house together. Almost immediately, she found she was pregnant, and nine months later gave birth to Daniel Ducovny.

While Daniel was still little more than a toddler, Meg became pregnant again, and as her body grew bigger and bigger, it became obvious that the walk-up apartment they had wasn't going to be large enough for the family. Before the birth of their second child, the Ducovnys moved to Eleventh Street, a place with enough space for them all. It was still on the Lower East Side, the same old neighborhood where Amram and Meg felt comfortable.

Then, on August 7, 1960, David William Ducovny was born.

As a baby and young child, David was very quiet and introspective. His older brother used to tease him for his silence in front of his friends, calling David "retarded" (David has his revenge these days by saying that Danny, who's a director of commercials in Los Angeles, "works with handicapped children"). In fact, he was anything *but* retarded. He was definitely shy, even after another child, his sister Laurie, was born when he was seven, but he was quick, intelligent, and alert.

There was often music around the apartment—Amram was a big fan of the late jazz singer Billie Holiday—and plenty of sports for the father and both sons. Amram was a pitcher on a softball team, and encouraged the boys to play as well, which David did. In fact, he discovered that he could lose himself in sports, and became accomplished at baseball, basketball, and swimming.

The children didn't see too much of their father, though. He was at work all day, and once he'd arrived home and eaten dinner, much of his evening was spent writing. This was for himself, to make his own mark on the world. He tried both books and plays, usually with a decidely political theme. When David was seven, Amram's play, *The Trial of Lee Harvey Oswald* had a short off-Broadway run. That was a big deal, real success, and naturally the whole family went to see it.

"It was *really* long," David recalled much later. "Oswald just sat there and didn't say anything the whole first act. I remember asking my father how it was possible that he didn't have to go to the bathroom."

Seeing people onstage, acting, didn't stir young David towards the profession. That would take almost twenty more years. Even his own first turn on the boards, playing one of the Magi in a fifth-grade nativity pageant, didn't whet his appetite for theater.

The brief success kept Amram Ducovny writing, but he turned his attention from the stage to the page, producing political books like *David Ben–Gurion in His Own Words* and *The Wisdom of Spiro T. Agnew*. He was disappearing more and more into his own world, causing a rift between himself and Meg. They tried to hide it from the children, but as things worsened it had to come into the open.

In 1972, when David was eleven, the couple divorced. It was a huge, unexpected shock to the boy. Danny was old enough to understand, and Laurie too young. But David was at the most susceptible age.

"The divorce was probably the most important emotional moment in my growing up," he told *Details.* "You are forced into an adult world of emotions that you aren't prepared to deal with. Your parents are trying to explain to you what has gone wrong with adult love. . . . They're talking about love that can go away. You're afraid it might go away from *you.* So it can define the way you deal with love for the rest of your life."

Like so many children in similar situations, David believed that he was the cause of the break-up. He'd been trying for a long time to learn how to whistle, in imitation of his father. Finally, just as he turned eleven, he discovered how to make the sound, and began doing it all the time, the way kids do with something they've just mastered, perfecting it and showing it off.

Needless to say, it was annoying to adults. And one day, David recounted, his father said, " 'Will you stop that infernal whistling?' I thought my father left because of my whistling."

Of course, that had nothing to do with it. Amram Ducovny was in his mid-thirties. He wanted to write, to live the romantic life so many people believed that writers lived, and that was impossible when you were working five days a week and coming home every night to a wife and three kids on the Lower East Side, just to force yourself to spend more hours at a desk, pushing your tired brain to produce more words.

If he didn't follow his desire now, he thought, he never would. Time would slip away. He'd become old, it would become too late, and all he'd be left with would be a life of regrets and "what ifs."

It was never an easy choice—abandon his dreams or abandon his family. He just didn't think he could have them both. So he did what he believed was the right thing, and followed his dream.

In fact, he followed it all the way to Paris, the city where Hemingway, Stein, Joyce, and so many others had made great literature in the past. The city of existentialism and sidewalk cafés, where a man could really live. And he did continue to write and publish more political books like *On With the Wind*, which was about Martha Mitchell, who was the wife of President Nixon's Attorney General at the time of the Watergate scandal. Maybe, in reality, things were a little different for Amram. He'd made his choice. He was the one who had acted.

For his family, though, it was as if some huge axe had fallen, and life had separated into two parts—before and after the divorce. Now Meg was responsible for everything. There was no salary coming in every month. She had to earn money *and* look after her children. It was a tall order.

"I got my iron from my mother," David said,

and it was easy to believe. Meg needed plenty of it to cope all alone. She'd trained as an elementary school teacher, and now that was how she supported her family.

Wracked with his feelings of guilt, the divorce made David even quieter and shyer. It became harder to get to know him, and friends were fewer. But the experience also gave him something new—a drive to succeed academically. He applied himself to his studies, which was wonderful for Meg, who was "afraid we'd all end up in the gutter."

Schoolwork didn't stop him from playing sports, however. Basketball remained a passion, and it was one that got him injured. Going up for a ball one day, his right eye was cut, badly enough to go to the hospital for treatment, leaving him with a pupil that would never fully contract.

By the time he was thirteen, David had managed to win himself a scholarship to Manhattan's prestigious Collegiate Preparatory School. He'd applied before and almost made it, but was rejected in the end in favor of another boy, the much better-connected John F. Kennedy, Jr..

Collegiate Prep was a place for the sons of the wealthy, a fast track to quality education and Ivy League schools. To graduate from there meant success. It wasn't the kind of place where kids from the Lower East Side who lived on one small income generally went. But David was in, and he was determined to excel among the children of the rich and famous.

The fact that he was there on a scholarship meant that he always had to try harder, put in that extra ounce of effort, and be the very best in everything he did. So his academic work was always excellent, and the talent he'd shown at sports soon had him playing baseball and basketball for the school.

The shy boy, growing awkwardly ('I never went through a really butt-ugly awkward stage,' he told *Seventeen*, "but I had my moments of *nearing* butt-ugliness. Like, my nose grew first, and, you know, it took a while for the rest to catch up. . . . I had my share of zits, too"), did manage to find a few friends in the school, classmates like Jason Beghe and Billy Wirth (who, curiously, also both became actors), and new interests, such as a passion for music.

Like most teenagers, his musical tastes ran all over the place. The first record he bought was a 45, "Grazing in the Grass," by the Friends of Distinction. But soon he was discovering the soul of Sly and the Family Stone, and, as adolescence bloomed, the complex progressive rock of Yes, whom he discovered "back when I was smoking pot in high school."

Although he was something of a wallflower, one thing David did very early was lose his virginity. As he explained to *Cosmopolitan*, "My buddy was twelve when he lost his, which I'm not condoning. For two long years, he taunted me, so I felt like the oldest virgin on the planet. I was anxious to get it over with. My virginity was a burden."

But that was a high point in David's teenage connection with girls. While he was at school, he never really dated, too shy to ask the girls he saw and liked to go out, and most of the time too focused on succeeding to even think about them.

Duke, as David had become nicknamed at Collegiate, still had his high academic goals. He wanted, and expected, to get into one of the Ivy League schools. It would show his classmates that the kid who commuted from the Lower East Side every day was just as good as they were with all their money. It would prove something to his father, in a way that David didn't really understand. And it would make his mother very proud.

As for himself, David wasn't thinking about that too much. He enjoyed studying, he was very good at it, particularly the liberal arts, and going to college seemed a lot better than going out and getting a job. He could have a career in academia, go from student to teacher and never have to deal with the real world.

So, although he smoked a little pot, he never let that pleasure get in the way of the work he had to do, or the sports he wanted to play. Those things were his ticket to bigger and better things, and nothing crazy was going to ruin it. Jason Beghe, who remained a close friend, said, "I was the gregarious one. David was the one who applied himself."

As a teenager at Collegiate, his distinctive sense of humor also began to develop. He'd always been shy and reserved. Now he began to find he could keep people at arm's length by being funny. Amram had had a strong sense of irony, which David had inherited or absorbed to a degree. To that he added a dry, sarcastic style, the perfect, slightly sophisticated mask to hide behind for someone who wasn't too sure of himself. He wanted to belong, in a way, to be part of a group. But for so many reasons, he never quite felt like he fit in, rather, that he was socially on the outside of everything.

When the time came to apply for college, David already had a short list of places that would be acceptable to him—the best schools, the names that were instantly recognizable. After five years of sweating at Collegiate, he felt he had a good chance, even if, unlike most of his classmates, there wasn't the family money to support him. His record, both scholastically and athletically, was strong enough to warrant a scholarship.

So being accepted by Princeton was, he felt, nothing more than his due, his reward for all the work he'd put in. It was the first step on the path he'd already mapped out, one his mother would approve of, taking him from undergraduate, to graduate student, to professor. Safe in the ivory tower and isolated from the world, but still using his brain every day. In other words, perfect for David Duchovny—who'd gone back to using the traditional spelling of his family's last name.

TWO

Menu Choice:
Advance

If Collegiate Prep had seemed snooty to David, it was nothing compared to the world he encountered at Princeton. Of course, he arrived in the fall of 1978, at a time when the idea of preppy fashions was sweeping America, making those places where it had begun and been a natural way of life—the Ivy League colleges and the expensive schools which fed them—become even more extreme in dress and attitude.

"I discovered what preppy really was," he remembered in *Entertainment Weekly*, "a level of Biff-dom I'd never seen before."

As part of mapping out his future, David had already decided what his major would be—literature. Words, and the worlds they could create, fascinated him, as did taking books apart to understand them, to unravel their power and meaning, the way the author had created a certain effect. Something about it clicked perfectly with him.

Of course, the fact that he was extremely intelligent helped. But David discovered he had a natural ability at literary criticism at the college level, which proved to be a far cry from the work he'd undertaken at Collegiate.

Princeton also finally brought him out of his shell a little bit. He contributed to the verbal cut and thrust in classes that he was taking, and realized that his opinion was as valid as anyone else's, sometimes more so. So, even in social situations, he began to talk more.

"I think when I was younger," he said in *Details*, "I wanted to tell everybody everything, because I thought I was so damn interesting." As he quickly learned, though, his opinions weren't always welcome ("Then I heard the snoring").

"I was really a tight-assed kind of student," was David's later opinion of himself. And certainly he had his own, very structured view of the world, where certain things—mostly the intellectual—counted, and others came much lower on the scale. When he learned that one of his roommates had ambitions to become an actor, David laughed at him.

"You came to Princeton," he said. "Why are you acting?"

Given the way things would turn out, it would prove to be quite an ironic question.

Just as he had at Collegiate, David buckled down and applied himself at Princeton. Work occupied much of his time, but he also had space for sports and some socializing. Doggie, as he came to be called, felt comfortable there, debating obscure points from a text he was reading or a theory of literary criticism. Using his mind was a pleasurable exercise, and this, he believed, was the ideal way to use it.

"The critical mind is a creative mind," he said. "There are books of criticism that are more enjoyable than the books they're criticizing."

Founded in 1746, Princeton has long been among the elite of colleges in America, one of the Ivy League schools famous for producing many of the top thinkers, academics, and politicians in the country. Only Harvard, William and Mary, St. John's, and Yale were older, and like those schools, Princeton had an effect on the history of America, with graduates like Presidents James Madison and Woodrow Wilson, former FBI head John Foster Dulles, and innumerable others.

Going there didn't take David too far from home—only to central New Jersey, far enough from New York to feel the distance, but close enough to visit regularly if he wanted.

Naturally, Meg was proud of her son for

what he'd achieved. And she firmly believed he had the capability to go all the way, to get his PhD and begin teaching. Education was the watchword she'd drummed into all three of her kids, and David seemed to have really taken it to heart.

But while he found that he could still excel academically, the athletic ability he'd been so proud of at Collegiate was pretty much worthless at the college level. The guys who played basketball there were taller, faster, much more aggressive. They *meant* it; this wasn't a pickup game in the schoolyard or the gym; they were serious. Finding his status as a player much lower than he'd always believed was something of a shock for David. Being among the best in everything he chose to do had been important to him ever since his parents' divorce, and now a little bit of that was being taken away from him. It was a rude introduction to the competitiveness of the adult world.

Overall, his four years at Princeton went very smoothly. As he'd suspected, the world of academia suited him perfectly, offering a life of reflection, exactly right for a young man who was still suffering from some shyness, who was more comfortable expressing himself on paper than in the flesh.

In the Class of '82, David graduated with a Bachelor of Arts in Literature. By then, though, he'd already been thinking a couple of steps ahead. Not for him the uncertainty of unemployment. He didn't want to be another liberal arts major hunting around for something he was qualified to do and finding nothing. He'd secured not just admission to Yale to do postgraduate work leading to a doctorate, but an impressive fellowship as well.

The competition for places in Yale's graduate program was strong enough. To get one *and* a fellowship, which would take care of most of his expenses, and also give him a chance to work as a teaching assistant with freshman undergraduates, put him in a higher category altogether, and meant that he was on the fast track to academic success—the doctorate, an assistant professorship somewhere, publication, tenure, a quiet, solid, comfortable life. That was what he aimed and labored for, what had been his ambition. But now, coming closer to realizing it, niggling doubts began to speak to him. Was this the right thing after all? Where was the adventure, the joy? But even as they entered his head, he swept them away.

So, in the fall of 1982, David took his books and belongings to the Yale campus, and settled in for the long haul of work. He still wasn't far from home, but New Haven, Connecticut, like Princeton, could have been a different world. Now, as a graduate student, he was mixing with some of the cream of American academia, people with massive reputations. People like John Hollander, Jay Hillis Miller, Geoffrey

Hartman, and Harold Bloom, internationally known and respected as a critic. Bloom was David's principal teacher and taught him two vital lessons: that "life is unfair. People hate each other for no reason and love each other for no reason" and that "[the biblical hero] David had charisma and Moses didn't. God, being like a human God in the Old Testament and not like the perfect God of the New Testament, loved David because David was a star."

While David enjoyed the life of a graduate student, immersing himself in his discipline, and learning much more about the art and scope of literary criticism, he wasn't as thrilled by the people who surrounded him. According to his sister Laurie, "he always used to describe everyone there as gargoyles." As always, he never quite managed to feel as if he fit into the mold; he would always remain something of an outsider, an observer.

Still, he obtained his master's degree without any problems, and began to work towards his PhD, choosing as his thesis topic "Magic and Technology in Contemporary Poetry and Prose," a subject which offered him full rein to explore the way modern writers—and their audiences—looked at science within the context of literature. Many people, although technology has been fully integrated into their lives (the microwave oven, the remote control), have no idea how it works. It retains a mystery that's akin to magic or alchemy.

"Science is really poetry," David explained to *Details*. "It's like a found poem. Incredible concepts, like the Heisenberg [Uncertainty] principle, are amazingly poetic. . . . I think Heisenberg was trying to observe the reactions of subatomic particles and basically the principle he came up with, the uncertainty principle, is really a poem and a philosophy of life, too: You cannot observe something without changing it."

But just as the path ahead was looking very straight, the occasional doubts David kept pushing away really began to grow and bloom.

"I was never fully convinced that I was meant to be an academic," he admitted later. Into his nineteenth year of school, it was perhaps a little strange to begin feeling those emotions, but they kept nagging away at him. The intellectual company around him began to seem sterile and boring. Still, he wasn't about to throw it all away for nothing. What he needed was an outlet.

He found one—and the start of a whole new career—by taking a class in playwriting at Yale Drama School. Initially he did it because he thought it would help his insight and writing for his thesis. But soon he began to enjoy it for its own sake. Before he realized it, drama and acting had crept under his skin, and he spent much of his free time at the drama school, hanging out with the acting students. They were a much looser bunch than the people he was around every day, more carefree. Still bright (they were at Yale, after all), but funnier, less serious about life. And David began to realize that he'd been missing a lot. His calling—the world of literature—might have been high, but it had left him in a sort of social isolation.

It had also kept him away from women.

While that hadn't seemed like such a big deal before, at twenty-five his hormones were really kicking into high gear. And acting, he suddenly realized, looked like a good way to meet women, the type of women he didn't come across in literature seminars—more glamorous, outgoing, sexier. The student who'd gone from deriding actors was now spending almost all his free time around them, and even tremulously treading the boards himself. As soon as he did that, the last vestiges of his old prejudices vanished. He *liked* it. It felt right, somehow, as if the pieces of his life were falling into place. It was thrilling, and it was fun. But he was determined it would just remain a sideline.

Jason Beghe, who'd been David's closest friend since their days together at Collegiate Prep, had become an actor. He kept encouraging David to explore acting more deeply, and it wasn't long before he was making occasional trips down to New York to take classes at The Actors Studio, a famous acting school, to see what was happening on the small stages around the city, and think about perhaps becoming more involved himself.

But while acting was rapidly becoming his avocation, his world still revolved around literature, the schedule of classes, seminars, and papers that ran his life. The only problem was that, with each passing week, it was becoming less and less satisfying. He'd had a glimpse of a world that existed outside his ivory tower, and he wanted to explore it.

To his own surprise, David discovered that he had real talent as an actor, something he'd never suspected. Performing scenes he could be "completely swept up in the emotions of acting and the extraordinary things that, as an actor, I could do." Seeing this side of his own personality, these things he'd never known existed inside himself, was a revelation, both liberating and terrifying. It opened him up, after he'd been very carefully clammed up his entire life. More than that, though, it worked as a kind of therapy for him.

"I realized I can have all these emotions, and I don't have to suffer from them," he said.

Still, he didn't entertain the idea of becoming an actor himself. He had his life, and this was a very fulfilling adjunct to it. However much as Jason suggested that he go along and audition for this or that, David refused. The doubts about the satisfaction of an academic career might still have been growing, but to stake everything on acting was a move to the other end of the spectrum, one he wasn't ready to make, or even consider too seriously.

"He made the decision to become an actor in increments," was the way Maggie Wheeler described it. She and David dated in the mid-eighties, and she saw how his mind slowly changed. "He'd put so much energy into academics and been so successful at it—switching to acting was a *big* deal."

It was such a big deal that it took him two full years to make the giant leap, two years where he continued work towards his doctorate. In fact, by 1987 all he had left to do was write his thesis.

But Jason kept calling, and finally David gave in and went along to an audition with him. It wasn't for a play or a movie. Not even for a television drama or comedy, but a commercial for Lowenbrau beer. It didn't aspire to great art, it was simply a way to sell a few more brews.

There was no reason David shouldn't get the part, Jason insisted. He could act, he was good-looking—in fact, he'd grown into quite the hunk. But if he didn't try, he'd never know if he could do it.

He got the part.

It wasn't much, really, playing a goofball in a

bar, tossing pretzels and catching them in his mouth.

"I was so nervous," he said later, "I felt awful for the people who hired me."

But when he saw the finished product, when he watched himself, it created an explosion in David's world. He'd been paid for acting. He began to realize that there was a possibility, however small, that he could make money, and have some fun, doing this.

Money seemed a very real possibility after the ad aired on television. On the basis of the clip, he was flown out to Los Angeles during Yale's Christmas break to test for three different television pilots. It was the kind of life that appeared in magazines—put up at the Sunset Marquis Hotel, whisked around the city by limo—not bad for someone with only one brief appearance, and a non-speaking role at that! With things backlogged over the holiday season, though, his Hollywood visit dragged on longer than expected, into the next semester. So David did the only thing he could in the situation—he called in sick to school. From the side of the pool at the hotel. It was a perfect L.A. moment, and the kind of thing that could turn anyone's head.

Although he didn't end up with any of the parts he tested for, the experience made him realize that acting could really work for him.

He decided to take the plunge.

When he told his mother that he was dropping out of school to become an actor, she was shocked.

"My mom was disappointed," he admitted. After all, he was *so* close to his PhD, to a degree that would really mean something. However, having made up his mind, David wasn't about to let himself be dissuaded. It was something he had to try, and *this* was the time to do it.

Just because David was suddenly ready to go for it, though, didn't mean that the world was about to roll over and declare him an instant star. Instead he found himself like every other aspiring actor, struggling, attending endless auditions, acquiring an agent, having photos taken, and spending a lot of time shuffling between dead-end jobs (in David's case, usually as a bartender) and the unemployment line, wondering if he'd made the right choice after all. There was the solace of the occasional small part in an off-Broadway (and off-off-Broadway) production, another line for the resume, but by and large, as he admitted, "That was probably the hardest time of my life."

Still, after the rigid, structured world of academia, this was freedom. Not perfect, and certainly not lucrative, but still exciting, even when he ended up wondering why he was doing it, and even if he should be doing it, if he really did have the talent. He tried out for any number of film parts, not getting a single one, until his agent called and suggested that he go down to an open call for work on a new movie that was shooting in Manhattan.

THREE

Formatting: Career

Working Girl was director Mike Nichols' take on America in the 1980s, when Reaganomics was the vogue and Wall Street was the land of monetary opportunity. It starred Melanie Griffith as a secretary from Staten Island who wanted to become a financial broker, and who saw the opportunity when her new boss (Sigourney Weaver) was laid up with a broken leg.

Posing as a broker, Griffith teamed up with a man from another firm (Harrison Ford) to put an elaborate deal together, only to have Weaver attempt to snatch all the credit away on her return.

In the end, however, the good gal triumphed. Weaver was disgraced, Griffith was promoted, and ended up with Ford.

As a comedy it dealt with the ideas of greed in the post-junk-bond era, and the way that America, for all it might deny it, really did have a class structure—fairly sophisticated concepts for a mass-market movie. But it made its points sharply, without ever belaboring them, managing to appear both worldly and gritty at the same time.

Working Girl was where David began his movie career. However, trying to find him in the film is a virtually impossible task, given that he appeared more or less only as an extra. There was no speaking part, no more than a second on-screen. But he was in a movie, and he'd been paid to be there. It was a beginning.

Still, it wasn't exactly the heights he'd aspired to when he quit Yale. And though he knew he'd have to start on the ground floor as an actor, he'd hoped for something a little more substantial as his first step along the acting road. So, after his very brief, distant glimpse of the spotlight, it was back to tending bar at night and spending the day pounding the pavement, going from audition to audition, and constantly checking his machine in hopes of receiving callbacks or offers.

When one finally came, it was hard to believe. After hearing "No, thank you," or simply nothing for so long, to actually get a part, and a fairly substantial part at that, was amazing, and a welcome relief to someone whose two appearances so far had been almost anonymous.

Director Henry Jaglom was part of the American film underground. Every few years he'd reappear with a new movie, something well removed from the mainstream, which would play in art houses around the country and in Europe to excellent reviews, but make next to no money. Since the films were often underfinanced in the first place, he lived very much on an artistic and commercial edge.

Not that he was a complete unknown, by any means. *Can She Bake A Cherry Pie?* had done moderately well, even being shown on cable TV. But Jaglom had no wish to go Hollywood. The money might be there, but he much preferred to pursue his own, unique vision without studio interference.

It was a trade off—money vs. independence—and Jaglom had no doubts about which side he was on.

He found a kindred spirit in David. Both were very bright, quirky, articulate men. For all that he needed money, David was enough of an intellectual to want to be involved in projects that appealed to something better than the lowest common denominator. But really, by now he was eager, even desperate, to be involved in *any* project at all, and to know that he did have a chance as an actor.

Jaglom's new film was *New Year's Day*. As with his previous work, it wasn't aimed at the multiplex audience. He viewed film as a way to explore feelings and issues, usually through conversation. That generally made his films too slow-paced for mass audiences, who wanted their entertainment fast-paced and exciting—in other words, utterly unlike their own lives.

Jaglom played Drew, a writer living in California. After his divorce, needing a change, he decided to return to New York, the city of his birth, in an attempt to find some new direction for his life.

Leaving Los Angeles on New Year's Eve, flying on the red-eye, he arrived on New Year's Day. When he got to the apartment he'd rented, he found it still occupied by three women.

Drew understood that his tenancy began on the first. The women believed that their lease ran through the first—so they hadn't yet moved out. Exhausted, Drew wasn't in much of a mood to fight about the matter. He tried to call hotels, but they were all full. The women—Winona (Melanie Winter), a photographer, Lucy (Maggie Jakobson), who provided voices for cartoons, and Annie (Gwen Welles), a publicist for an art gallery—offered to let him stay there, and he agreed.

What he ended up observing, as he tried to rest, wasn't so much their packing as their lives in motion.

Winona was eager to become a mother, a willing single parent.

Annie, neurotic and edgy, was scared of the change after four years of sharing a place with the same people, her friends.

And Lucy, the center of the film, was reversing Drew's journey, heading west to Los Angeles, to make her own escape after discovering Billy's (David Duchovny's) faithlessness to her.

It was David's big break, the thing every aspiring actor could wish for. There was plenty of screen time, some good close-ups, a fair amount of dialogue, and even, within the framework of the film, a character who was well-developed. Billy might not have been a particularly nice guy, and he was certainly lacking in the area of commitment, but David had a chance to talk at length, and proved he was comfortable improvising (much of the film was unscripted).

His laid-back, somewhat laconic style was quite evident in a long scene with Jaglom, as Billy admitted his failings, ones which perhaps also applied to David himself. Billy was a Lothario; he liked the idea of being with one woman, but found it impossible not to pursue every one he saw. For David, "I do believe in monogamy. Some people have it in their bones, it's their calling. But for others, including me, staying monogamous requires constant vigilance."

The fact that David's then-girlfriend, Maggie Jakobson, was playing his girlfriend in the movie only added to the emotional sparks that flew in the scenes between them. But even then, David didn't emote, or raise his voice. That just wasn't his manner. He stayed low-key, very understated, not too obvious. It was, really, an ideal modern acting style, one which hardly seemed like acting at all. You had to watch him very closely to see what was going on, the way he allowed things to slowly build.

"Unfortunately," he said, "we live in a time when people don't watch too closely. They want someone to jump out and grab them." And that wasn't a style he was about to start using.

There was no way on earth that *New Year's Day* was going to make an instant success out of David. The film was simply too marginal, seen by small audiences in America and Europe. Nonetheless, he said, "My agent thought I should move to California in case there was any 'heat' when *New Year's Day* opened. And there *was* a little heat, but the only thing that happened was that I changed agents."

In the end, his big break came and went fairly quietly. The heat, which had been tepid at best, quickly died, and David was stuck on the West Coast, still unknown, and a few thousand miles from all that was comfortable to him.

FOUR

Macro
Connections

A year can be a very long time in an actor's life. Certainly for David, the period between moving to Los Angeles and finding real acting work seemed to drag out forever. He was in the right place for a career in movies and television, attending all the auditions his agent sent him on, but nothing was happening.

He had the looks and the body; there was no doubt of that. But in southern California, in the acting field, so did everyone else. And in the bright sun, his darkness worked against him. His coloring, his manner, even his acting style, exuded a certain brooding quality, an introspection which didn't work too well in the land of the toothpaste smile and the shallow emotion.

What it meant was that when a job finally did come his way, it would be in something that was every bit as unconventional as a Henry Jaglom film.

"Twin Peaks" was film director David Lynch's attempt to subvert television. Lynch, who'd honed his somewhat skewed vision of the world in *Eraserhead, Blue Velvet,* and *Wild at Heart,* had been given carte blanche to develop a series.

What ensued made TV history. As macabre as anything he'd put on the big screen, albeit toned down a little, it began with a body, and moved on through there to explore the character of the town of Twin Peaks, Washington (the actual outdoor shooting took place in Snoqualmie, Washington), and its inhabitants, who were, at least through Lynch's eyes, a remarkably strange bunch.

For the critics, the show seemed like a godsend, something with substance placed in the arid wasteland of prime-time programming. And Lynch's reputation promised the bizarre, which he delivered in spades. But a two-hour film is utterly different from a weekly series. While "Twin Peaks" worked in the short term, initially attracting viewers through the critical interest it had received, it soon ran out of steam—and worthwhile ideas. What had been strange and exotic became to many people odd and labored, and ratings dropped. While a core of fans remained, mostly those who'd followed Lynch's work for years, the vast majority of people turned their attention—and their remotes—elsewhere.

By the time David joined the show, it was already on its last legs, staggering towards oblivion. After the early surge, it had become a cult item, and those didn't pay the bills.

David's casting was very much a last-minute deal. He ended up with a day and a half to prepare for his role, the first—but definitely not the last—time he'd portray a lawman.

Not just any DEA agent, though. As Dennis/Denise Bryson, David definitely had a chance to get in touch with his feminine side, and find out how comfortable bras and pantyhose really were. He was the type of law enforcer who would either make J. Edgar Hoover roll over in his grave, or jump for joy, depending on what you believe about the former FBI head.

Presenting himself to the television masses in dresses and high heels didn't really bother David. No one knew who *he* was. And, as he pointed out, "I didn't have a career to ruin at that point, really . . . It was such a cool part in such a cool show, even though it was on the decline, everyone was overjoyed I got the job. I was nervous because I didn't know how to do it, didn't know how to prepare."

Given the nature of the part, and the show,

there was very little preparation he could have done, other than to use a depilatory on his legs and discover what size dresses to wear.

Certainly finding clothes that would fit proved to be a problem for the wardrobe department. In the end the only bra they could come up with that would even fasten around his chest was the one plump German actress Marianne Sagebrecht had worn in the movie *Baghdad Cafe*. And that was hardly a perfect fit.

It gave David an appreciation of what women have to go through every day.

"My bra was cutting into my skin!" he sympathized later. "You poor women. Men just throw on a pair of jeans."

Since, with some professional help in make-up and hair styling, he looked quite convincing as Denise, it wasn't too surprising that some of the staff on the show thought he really *was* a transvestite, and ended up laughing at him behind his back.

"The interesting thing," he mused, "is that it hurt my feelings. I have been lucky or unlucky enough to be an accepted human being. I'm white, I'm male, I'm straight. Now I know the constraints women feel when they dress, what it's like to be ridiculed for being gay by unfeeling men. And on top of that," he added slyly, "my vanity kicked in. I felt so unattractive."

His performance as the DEA agent who spent his free time in drag might have shocked America, if America had still been watching

"Twin Peaks." By the time he appeared though, in all of three episodes in 1991, it was simply a case of titillating the faithful, nothing particularly outrageous by the standards Lynch had set in his movies.

Still, it was a great clip for David to add to his resume. The show got plenty of publicity over the course of its run, some directed at David's character. His name might have been forgotten, but people in the industry knew exactly who he'd played. It was the greatest share of the spotlight he'd received yet, and after a discouraging first year in Los Angeles, it was enough to convince him to stay.

Which was just as well. Major success wasn't waiting *right* around the corner, but his career, which had seemed stalled a step past square one, was beginning to take off. Not rapidly, but enough to convince him that he hadn't made the wrong choice after all.

In his free time—which was still most of his time—David had started writing poetry, and attending the poetry readings which had sprung up like artistic weeds in the coffeehouses and bars around Los Angeles. After all, he'd studied literature, he had a master's degree in the subject, and the space to reflect and put his thoughts on paper. Hearing people spout their verse helped pass the empty hours.

He was ready and available for any and every part that came his way. He wanted—he *needed*—to work, to pay his bills, build up his resume, get some momentum going. The next role didn't exactly forward his career, but it did offer some money for a little—very little, really—work.

Rob Lowe and James Spader were the stars of *Bad Influence*, which desperately wanted to be a dark, menacing film, the type which tumbled a fairly innocent hero (Spader) into the sort of hell he had no choice but to fight his way out of. Had it worked, it would have been great, but with its script and its leads there was never much chance of that. Sinister wasn't really part of Lowe's acting range, and while Spader was good at looking confused, he was never quite believable as a man of action.

David walked into all this for about a second. His credit read "Man in bar," and that was who he played. The camera panned past him, in his shades, looking cool and hip in a trendy club. And that was it. The sum total of his appearance in the movie. The most surprising thing was that it even warranted a credit at all. It was an extra's role. No words, not even a close-up.

But it was a paycheck, and it was better than spending his days at home or attending auditions. And the next one, he felt certain, would be better.

It was. *Julia Has Two Lovers* took him back to the realm of the independent art movie he'd entered when he worked for Henry Jaglom. Written by its star, Daphna Kastner, who'd also come up with the original story, it was a low-budget affair, but still well-shot, full of California light, and all the angst and confession only the West Coast or New York could generate.

Julia Michener (Kastner), a writer of childrens' books, lived with Jack (David Charles), the man who published her work. They'd been together for two years, and he wanted to marry her. She wasn't so certain, and kept postponing the decision, trying to make up her mind, while he pressed her for an answer.

Then Daniel (David) entered her life. It was, supposedly, a wrong number that he'd called. At least that was what he told her as they began to talk. They were both at home, alone, and somehow something clicked in the conversation.

Something like this was exactly what Julia needed. A warm, sympathetic man who wanted to hear all she wanted to say, who could be open with her, telling her all his secrets, showing her his past until she felt she knew him.

In turn, Julia opened up to him.

Julia and Daniel talked all day. The phone became their world. He wanted to meet her, to make love to her, to make this a reality. And she wanted him, too. The freedom to speak that he'd given her had made him fall in love with her. She invited him over for lunch the next day.

When he arrived, he was all she could have hoped for.

They made love, and then slept.

While Julia dozed, Daniel dressed and left. She didn't have his address or his phone number. Believing he had left her for good, Julia hunted him down. After a confrontation between Jack and Daniel, Jack left and Daniel asked Julia to marry him.

But Julia had done a great deal of thinking in the last two days. What she needed for the moment was some time alone, to think things through and to become used to this new freedom, to let herself expand to fill the apartment she now occupied by herself. She told Daniel to call her in a few weeks.

Would he? Could he hold on that long? Was it in him? Those were the answers the audience would never find out.

Julia Has Two Lovers had its moments, but they were few and far between. Julia was neurotic, Jack kept himself wound up so tight he might have burst, and Daniel was a person who lived on strange ideas.

But the way David played him, with a certain goofy, aloof charm, worked perfectly. He was the only one of the three who didn't come across as self-conscious on the screen; then again, Daniel was meant to be a person who operated more on instinct than rational thought.

And once again, in a sort of "dream sequence," David got to show off his body, standing on Julia's balcony, partly-hidden by net curtains which blew in the wind. It continued what would seem to become a fairly regular trend in his films.

Even though it was an independent film, playing such a strong role in it—and doing it so well—could only help David's career. *New Year's Day* had given him his first real chance, and "Twin Peaks" had shown he was capable of working in a very professional situation. This illustrated how he could develop a character, take the words from the page and build them into a living, breathing whole. It was far more than another line on his resume, really; it was a turning point. Daphna Kastner had given him the chance to really do some work, and he'd run with it. He was believable as a person with the odd impulses to call up women at random, as someone who could charm them into staying on the line, and as a very sensual man. That was more than getting by on his looks; that was real talent.

The low-key style he'd been developing was the trick, as much as any trick was involved. David made Daniel sound natural—not emoting too much, not trying to grab scenes, but just easing slowly from one thing to the next. Overall the film didn't have too much to recommend it—the idea itself was unlikely, and Julia needed to be played by someone with more acting ability than Daphna Kastner to be fully convincing. But if the movie offered only one great thing, it was the blossoming of David's talent. And that made it more than worthwhile.

For the first time he was really able to sink his teeth into a part. Dennis/Denise Bryson had been interesting for him, but it had been, literally, all facade. Daniel stripped that away and let him show more of what he could really do.

Unfortunately, his next role didn't give David the opportunity to capitalize on that. *Denial* was about the lasting effect a relationship had on a woman, Loon (Robin Wright). David didn't play the object of her obsessions, but rather John, one of a group of her friends in the late sixties or early seventies. There wasn't much for him to do beyond clown around and have one brief serious scene with Loon. Still, it paid the rent and entered another credit on the ledger. He was working, and that was the important thing. It cut down on the time he had to spend in the workaday world, and he was even managing to pay his rent with his acting—at least some of the time.

And some of the time would rapidly become most of the time. He'd barely finished work on *Denial* when he managed to snag another film role, his third in a year. Nineteen ninety-one was being good to him.

Don't Tell Mom the Babysitter's Dead was supposed to herald the start of a big movie career for Christina Applegate, the Lolita daughter on television's "Married With Children." Its biggest problem was that, as a comedy, it simply wasn't very funny. Applegate was fine as Sue Ellen Crandall, quite convincing as a teenager who learned to grow up very quickly. The problem was the script.

That, however, wasn't really David's concern. As Bruce, the slimy head inventory clerk in the company where Sue Ellen had bluffed her way into a job, he made the most of a few lines. Hair slicked back, he teamed up with Caroline, the receptionist whose promotion Sue Ellen had taken, to find out the truth about the mystery employee.

He might not have had much, but he hammed it up, relishing each word like a Victorian villain. Of course, being the bad guy, he was thwarted every step of the way, ending up with his just deserts, as the kids toilet-papered his car.

David proved to one of the movie's few bright spots. He made the most of the little he had to work with, in a role utterly unlike anything he'd done before, and it worked. Bruce was really memorable. It added to the range of what David could do. In real life he had a dry sense of humor—some had even called it sarcasm—but this was the first chance he'd had to show it on-screen. He could make it work for him. He had a natural sense of timing.

It had been fun to do something completely different from his past work, even if he ended up no more recognizable than before. Every bit of work added up. And sooner or later it would begin to pay off. When his agent sent him the script for *The Rapture*, David began to think that time might just be sooner.

FIVE

Press ESC.
to Recapture

Things were definitely beginning to look up for David. Since "Twin Peaks," he'd been able to find regular acting employment, even if it hadn't exactly stretched his talents as a thespian. But it was work, and in a field where most of the people were unemployed at any given time, he was definitely making headway. Every few months he was able to add another line to his resume, and have the gratifying feeling that he was making a living from his art, even if that living was just scraping by, rather than any lap of luxury.

To move ahead he needed to be seen, to show what he could really do, a role that would challenge him in a film that people would remember. That was the way to break out of the cycle of bit parts, hand-to-mouth existence, and constant worry.

He was working towards it. His confidence in his abilities had grown as he used them, and now he was going out and auditioning for larger roles. He wasn't getting them, but the spirit was there. He felt he was ready for them at last.

Although roles of any kind were what he needed, the academic in him still wanted to be involved in projects with some substance and intelligence. Films with real depth and fiber were the films that lasted, that people recalled, and that he'd be able to point to with pride in the years to come.

So when he received the script for director Michael Tolkin's movie, *The Rapture*, he was immediately intrigued.

"The Rapture" was a fundamentalist Christian term, a way of referring to the Day of Judgment, when God would return to earth, and all those who believed, who opened their hearts to Him, would be caught up in the Rapture and taken to heaven.

Now, that idea was as old as Christianity itself. But with the revival of religious fundamentalism in America, the question of faith, and its power over people, had become an issue worth exploring.

What truly set *The Rapture* apart, though, was its willingness to look at Christian fundamentalism seriously. People had been all too willing to skewer the religious right, to make fun of it and those who believed. This film took them seriously, treated them as real, serious human beings, people who believed with all their hearts and souls, and were tested.

It steered well away from the political rocks that could easily have capsized it, telling a story rather than preaching.

Mimi Rogers was the star of the film, continuing the interesting, sometimes offbeat work she'd done—another actor who could easily have become a major star, but who preferred the challenge of more difficult, if less glamorous roles.

This time out, David sidestepped the bit-part routine, and read for Randy, a strong supporting character. He might not have agreed with the premise of the movie, but it was different—different enough, and controversial enough, to be noticed. He was eager to be a part of it.

He walked away a happy man.

Mimi Rogers played Sharon, a Los Angeles telephone operator with a void in her life that she tried to fill with sex. At work she was professional and detached, but that detachment ran through her days and nights.

Sharon was keeping the world at arm's length.

One night she and Vic met Randy (David) and his girlfriend in a bar. Somehow, a small spark was ignited between Sharon and Randy.

They began spending nights together. He felt able to confide in her, telling her that he'd killed a man for money in 1975, and that his conscience had been bothering him ever since. But Sharon's dissatisfaction with her lifestyle was growing. She felt empty, she wanted something, but she had no idea what. At work she heard people talking about "The Pearl" and "The Boy"; she tried to join in, claiming to have dreamed of the pearl, but they knew she was lying. After a conversion experience, Sharon came home and tried to convert Randy.

Six years later Randy was forced to fire one of his employees. The man did what could never be foreseen—returned to the office with a shotgun and began killing people, including Randy. After seeing a sign, Sharon took her daughter into the desert. But when further signs didn't appear, Sharon lost faith and shoots her daughter, ending up in jail.

But as she sat in her cell, the first of six blasts from Gabriel's trumpet came. The bars crumbled and fell. Sharon knew what was happening, but she didn't move.

Sharon, given chance after chance, refused to believe. And when the final trumpet call came, she was left in a wasteland for all eternity.

It was the kind of film that produced strong reactions, both for and against. There was nothing subtle about it, and all too often the writing was ridiculously heavy-handed. But for a modern American movie out of Hollywood to

have the issue of faith at its center, well, that
was news in and of itself.

The critics enjoyed it. Maybe it wasn't the
best thing ever produced, but it made people
leave the theaters thinking and questioning
themselves and their beliefs.

As Randy, David was in less than half the
film, but the presence of his character lingered
over the whole movie. As always, in his style,
he underplayed, letting the picture of Randy
build gradually, in increments. Making *The
Rapture*, he said later, was "a difficult experience"—not so much for the technicalities, but
the subject matter.

His style on-screen was developing, a minimalist thing, letting the audience use its imagi-
nation, rather than hitting them over the head
with sweeps of emotion. And for this film it
was ideal. The story was strong and powerful
enough to carry the film; any overacting would
have seemed ridiculous. So David's casting was
perfect. The story of Randy having been a hit
man once, how it had preyed on his mind, had
all the more impact for being delivered
straightforwardly and thoughtfully. It really
sounded as if he'd spent many, many sleepless
nights turning the incident, with all its implications, over in his mind.

As Randy found God, the changes David
made to the character—other than the shorter
hair, and the suit replacing grubby denims—
were subtle. The rage and confusion vanished

from his eyes, replaced by serenity and smiles. There was a new air of patience and acceptance. Perhaps the greatest shame was that Randy had to be written out of the plot so early. This was, by far, the biggest break David had enjoyed, and he'd fine-tuned the character so exactly that he truly deserved more screen time, more exposure. Although, perhaps, the film *did* bring enough of that in one way. Once again, as in *New Year's Day*, David had a nude scene.

"I'm lucky enough to have an athletic body," he told *Cosmopolitan*, "and I work out, so being naked is fine. Sex scenes don't embarrass me, although there's a shot in *The Rapture* where you can actually see my . . . well, you know what I mean."

Once the movie opened, David had every right to expect bigger and better parts. He'd done outstanding work and shown that he was ready, and more than able, to handle big roles. His time, he knew, was coming. The leap to stardom had to be just around the corner.

But life didn't work quite that way for him. *The Rapture* wasn't followed by another co-starring role, then headlining in his own right, as it should have been. It turned out that being a co-star meant next to nothing in Hollywood in the '90s. Having your name high on the credit list carried no weight at all; you only mattered if your name was above the title.

So it was back home, waiting by the phone

for his agent to call, reading scripts for movies that might have been good or awful, but which didn't suit his style at all, and hoping for just the right vehicle to come along and electrify his career.

He was still going to the poetry readings he'd discovered after moving to Los Angeles. They'd become quite the trendy thing now, to the point where you could barely go into a coffee-house or a dark bar without someone standing in a corner and declaiming his work.

David had even toyed with the idea of reading himself. He was still writing poetry. He knew well enough that he wasn't an Ashberry, a Frost, or a Williams, but what he was putting on paper wasn't too bad. Certainly good enough for the people who seemed happy to listen to anything.

For a long time, though, reluctance won out. Acting was one thing. Even if you were making a character live, making him feel, there was still that mask to hide behind, and the words belonged to someone else. Up there, reading his own work, he'd be emotionally naked. And he wasn't quite certain he could do that.

Finally he did pluck up his courage, and took his work down to the Largo Pub on Fairfax Avenue. He'd been there often, just to hang out and hear other people read, most of whom were awful. But until that night he'd never indicated that he wrote himself. David had already decided what he was going to read by the time he left his apartment. All his life he'd felt a bit of an outsider, first at school, then at the colleges he'd attended, and now as an actor. He wanted to belong, but couldn't. He always stood at the entrance, the threshold, not quite in, but not out, either. That was the subject of his poem.

Like most good poetry, it worked on more than one level. It was also written to a woman he'd been seeing. Like him, she was a threshold person. And that was why their relationship had absolutely no chance of working; neither of them could get beyond the doorway and into the room, to make that commitment.

She was at the Largo that night, sitting through the other readers, waiting for David. When he'd finished, he asked for her response to his work. She came up with one word: "Hmmm."

Others, though, were pleasantly astonished. Whatever they'd been expecting from him, this wasn't it.

"People were surprised that I could write," he remembered. "There's a certain charge in the room and you know when people are with you, and when they're thinking, 'When's the next guy coming up?'"

The favorable response didn't fill David with an overwhelming desire to abandon acting and turn to poetry full-time. He was too involved for that. Nor did it do much to advance his relationship with the woman. But it did leave a feeling of satisfaction. Acting was one way of purging himself of emotion; this was another. An outlet, a release valve. He could put it all down on paper, and, if he wanted, read it out loud somewhere.

And with the frustration he felt towards his career, release was important. Yes, he'd been working consistently, he had a decent roof over his head, he wasn't starving, but progess was so slow. David was enough of a realist to know that stardom was as much about luck as talent, but his numbers didn't seem to be coming up on the dice. He'd take a step ahead, and that would be it. There should have been more.

He believed—he knew—he had ability as an actor, even if his style wasn't as flashy as others. Although it wasn't especially important to him, he knew he had the looks and the body necessary to make it in Hollywood. But however many sparks he generated, the fire never quite started.

He needed to work, to do anything, even a return to bit parts, just to keep himself busy, to keep the brooding at bay. Most of all, he needed something light and fun, a chance to spread the comedy wings he'd shown the year before. So, when he was offered a part in a family comedy—playing someone just as oily and sleazy as Bruce in *Don't Tell Mom the Babysitter's Dead*—he jumped at the opportunity.

SIX

New Program
Object: Breakout

After *The Rapture* it might have been a giant step backwards, but that didn't really matter. It was work, involvement, and a paycheck. And while dogs have figured largely in David's life in the last few years (he's accompanied by one in "Red Shoe Diaries" and he has his own dog, Blue, for company in Vancouver), *Beethoven* was the only time he'd had one starring over him.

It was the kind of movie that Disney had done so well in the 1960s, family entertainment which mixed adventure and comedy, with the kids as heros, the pets humanly smart, and a happy ending to make everyone smile.

David played Brad, who with his wife, Brie (Patricia Heaton), were considering investing in

George Newton's auto-air-freshener business. With his double-breasted suit and his hair blow-dried into a sculpture, Brad was the archetypal evil yuppie, a complete phony from the top of his head to the tips of his expensive shoes, calling George "Giorgio" and using the ever-trendy "Ciao" as he left. You hated him, and her, from the moment you saw them; everything was as it should be.

After "crunching some numbers" Brad and Brie had decided that Newton Air Fresheners looked like a good investment. They were going to put $125,000 into the business, to help it expand and eventually become the biggest in the country. They wanted to go to a restaurant with the Newtons to celebrate; eventually a compromise was reached—they'd go to George and Alice Newton's for a barbecue.

Which was how they found themselves sitting around a table in the backyard, being stared at by the Newtons' kids—creatures Brad and Brie had no time for.

They were eager to have George sign, far too eager for Alice. She wanted him to take his time and review the paperwork. Only Beethoven, the family's St. Bernard, knew what was really going on. He'd heard Brad and Brie talking, letting slip that they'd own the company in six months—and of course he understood every word.

He wasn't about to let his family get swindled. When Brie made a fuss of him, he began to wind around the table and chairs, wrapping his leash around the metal legs.

Finally, his slobbering presence was too much for Brad, who threw a ball for him to fetch. Beethoven, of course, was only too happy to obey, and took off, taking the table and chairs—Brad and Brie still attached—on a jaunt through the neighborhood. Needless to say, they didn't bother sticking around for the contract.

It was a nicely wicked little role, just a few minutes of screen time, but memorable. David let himself overact for once, really hamming it up, and it was precisely what the part needed. Gestures, nicknames, it was all perfect. Even the hair, which looked like a helmet, was a lovely little parody. Though it was just a small part (his name was way down on the cast list), he made it count.

Not that the film didn't generate its own memories for him.

"Saint Bernard saliva is sticky and nasty," he said. "If you can imagine bad-smelling maple sap, that's what it's like to work with that dog."

And, as *Beethoven* proved to be a very popular movie with kids, a whole new audience got the see the comedic side of David. His timing was great and even when he was overacting, his understated manner made everything seem natural and unforced.

Although the critics savaged it, *Beethoven* was

a big hit with the family audience, making it one of the box office successes of 1992. Which left a certain wry irony in the fact that, before "The X-Files" made him into a huge star, David's most widely recalled scene was being dragged through bushes and over fences by a dog.

With *Beethoven* out of the way—and it didn't take too long to film that brief role in the movie—he needed work, work, and more work, anything and everything to get him noticed and push his career along. By now it was obvious that the boost which should have happened following *The Rapture* wasn't going to happen. He needed to make another break.

Unfortunately, *Ruby* wasn't it. It had all the earmarks of a classy production and was directed by John Mackenzie, who'd done such outstanding work on *The Long Good Friday* a few years before. It starred the excellent character actor Danny Aiello in the title role as Jack Ruby, the man who murdered Lee Harvey Oswald, the supposed assassin of John F. Kennedy, in 1963.

To say David was wasted in the part of Dallas Police Officer J.D. Tippit would be to put it mildly. With a total of three lines—actually, one real line of dialogue and two cheers—he didn't exactly have a lot to say. Yet, during the first part of the movie, his face appeared on-screen more than a few times.

It was almost as if there had been more, but

somewhere along the way his part ended up on the cutting-room floor. As it stood, there was no point in his character ever appearing, let alone talking. He did nothing to advance the plot, and the recurrent images of his face, looking more and more obsessed with the new dancer in Ruby's club, Candy Cane (Sherilynn Fenn, with whom David had worked on "Twin Peaks"), only served to mystify the audience.

About the only possible explanation is that, prior to editing, the film had contained a small sub-plot concerning a romance between Tippit and Candy, or the cop throwing himself at her in one way or another.

But that's only speculation. In the version released to theaters in 1992, David's appearance was of the blink-and-you-missed-him variety.

It was a rough stretch for David. No matter what he did, or how hard he tried, the bigger roles just seemed to evade him. He was working, yes, but he was in this business to act, to show what he could really do, not for a day or two at a time, but for the entire length of a movie. He wanted to be able to build a character, see him develop.

He'd always known it wasn't easy, that actors were a dime a dozen to directors—at least until you hit the jackpot. But that jackpot seemed far, far away at the moment.

Nor did his involvement in *Chaplin* look as if it would bring it any closer. Richard Attenborough's film, with its epic look at the life of Charlie Chaplin, was a star vehicle—but for Robert Downey, Jr., not David. While Downey was superb—he truly deserved every ounce of praise that came his way—David was relegated, not even to the co-star list, but the place he'd become used to, the smaller print of the secondary character list.

He played Rolly, Mack Sennett's cameraman in the early days of Hollywood, and he was a living stereotype with his cap on backward, cranking the camera by hand. Rolly became a friend of Chaplin's and a trusted aide, moving with him from Sennett to Chaplin studios, and working with him on the classic films of his career. That should have been enough to get David more than a miserly few lines of dialogue, but no. The continuation of their working relationship was shown by occasional glimpses of David, growing slightly older, and mustached, sitting with his boss, or nodding his approval at a piece of footage.

It wasn't the type of work that was going to leave him rich, famous, or even satisfied; but lately he hadn't had the opportunity to give enough of a performance even to be dissatisfied. And, in a vicious circle, his parts were so small that he wasn't getting mentioned in reviews, which made it harder to see casting directors and try out for the kind of parts that *would* help him make a name for himself.

It was enough to make him willing to return

to television. With the exception of "Twin Peaks" it was a medium he'd carefully avoided. Film acting was where his heart lay, and once someone was known for his work on the small screen, making the transition to the larger one was often difficult.

But beggars simply could not afford to be choosers. It probably wasn't anything David would have taken in ideal circumstances, but the chance of a featured role in the television movie "Babysnatcher" seemed just too good to refuse in 1992.

He played David Anderson, a married man having a secret affair with Karen Williams (Nancy McKeon), a divorced mother of two, who was close to her due date with a third child—David's baby.

Anderson was quite content to let things continue as they were. He had the best of both worlds, his own family at home, and Karen with her kids on the side. His wife, Anne, didn't know what was happening, and Karen wasn't putting any pressure on him to come and live with her, even after the baby was born.

But when the baby was kidnapped by a deranged woman (Veronica Hamel) trying desperately to keep her own marriage together, things changed fast. Anderson learned he wasn't going to be able to have his cake and eat it, too.

The police question Anderson, wondering if his wife might have snatched the child for revenge, or whether he, or even Karen, might have committed the crime.

Karen's focus shifted entirely to getting the child back safely. If Anderson wanted to help with that, fine. If not, then she didn't need him in her life any more.

He was forced to make some hard decisions. He was going through his own little hell, and no one was there for him. After being used to support from both sides, suddenly he had to work things out for himself.

He told Anne about the affair, moved into a motel, and began to work with Karen to find the baby. He wanted to be with her and with their new baby when they found her.

But the finding was proving difficult. It was only sheer luck that gave them a break, and brought the infant back unharmed.

Karen had discovered a lot during the ordeal. She'd found strengths she never knew she had, and the ability to cope alone, if necessary. Anderson was with her now, but as to the future, who could really tell?

Veronica Hamel was the top name, but it turned out to be Nancy McKeon's movie. She was the one with the presence and the force all the way through. David, again, had no more than a secondary role, and it was one that never really gave him much chance to project. His character spent all his time dithering, undecided about what he should do, and trying to avoid the consquences of his actions.

To be sure, it was easy to believe that Karen would fall for Anderson. He was good-looking, smooth without ever seeming slick. There was a warmth and solidity about him. In the crisis, though, that veneer vanished, and he became someone needy, flimsy, and obviously not fully committed.

But David worked with what he had—a fairly trite, clichéd script—and pushed hard to make the audience feel Anderson's confusion. Against the odds—he was a minor sub plot, after all, and therefore not especially important—he succeeded. He connected, rising above cheap emotions to real anguish. Whether or not you approved of Anderson, he seemed three-dimensional, and in real pain.

What was obvious was just how far David had come since his appearance in *New Year's Day*. In three short years all the amateurism had gone from his performance, hammered away by time and plenty of hard work. The innate talent had been honed. To be fair, this was mainstream television, which wanted to be polished, as opposed to independent film, which relied more on vision than formula, but David had made the transition from gifted amateur to real professional. His range had widened immensely. He'd developed a true presence on camera, with a face the lens enjoyed, a face that was taking on more and more character with each year of his maturity.

After *The Rapture* and this feature, it was becoming much easier to believe that David really would make it someday, that he'd break through the line of actors to stardom. All the qualities he could provide were in place now. Only two more things were needed—a little time and a lot of luck.

One thing he hadn't anticipated was more work in television. David still thought of it as something of a dead end in the career he'd mapped out for himself, even after "Baby-snatcher" had given him some exposure. But the new offer he received was to take part in a very different type of show.

Zalman King's credits as a director included *9½ Weeks* and *Wild Orchids,* both of which trod a fine line between mainstream films and adult cinema. Now he wanted to see how far he could extend that line on television. He'd contracted with Showtime, the cable network, to create a series called the "Red Shoe Diaries," which would push at the boundaries of sex on television. The show would be erotic, but not pornographic. And the stories would center on women—they would be the strong figures.

The concept was definitely intriguing. David was offered the role of Jake, the narrator of the series, a man who kept an ad running in a Los Angeles paper asking for letters from women who were "betrayers, or had been betrayed."

Those who wanted to reply had to write with their experiences to "Red Shoe." Jake, with his dog, would frame each tale with a brief introduction and conclusion.

The pilot episode, the one that convinced David that he really did want to be involved in this after all, was "Jake's Story," the story of how he ended up placing the ad, why he was always alone and so sorrowful.

"I didn't know where it was going to go," David said, "but the pilot was good."

Jake was a successful young architect in L.A., living with the girl he loved, Alex (Brigitte Bako), an interior designer. It was a very sensual, honest relationship. Neither of them held anything back. And that proved to be a problem for Alex, as she noted in her diary. She felt as if she needed a secret, something that was entirely hers, that Jake couldn't share. When she met Tom, a man who loved shoes and could guess a woman's size, she was plunged into a nightmare of infidelity and guilt.

At home, in the bath, Alex was at her wit's end. Tom had threatened to come to her home, which would mean that Jake would know everything. What had started out as fun had overwhelmed her. She took a razor and slit her wrists.

It was Jake who found her. He couldn't understand why she'd done it. They'd been so happy, they had such a bright future together. After the funeral he just fell apart. He ignored his work, stayed in the loft they'd shared, and slowly packed up her things.

Until he discovered the diary.

Then it all began to make sense. Jake follows Tom and challenges him to a game of basketball. When Tom learns who Jake is, a terrible fight ensues.

Finally Tom had to go to the bathroom to attend to the bloody nose Jake had given him. While he was there, the women left. Now it was just Jake and Tom, and time for some truth.

Jake laid it out, showing where Alex had died, tossing the pair of red shoes at him so there could be no mistake. And Tom made the only response he could make—he knocked Jake out. He'd loved Alex, too. It had been more than a quick fling to him. He'd wanted her to be with him.

The next day Jake placed his ad. The idea had come from a passage in Alex's diary, where she fantasized about hearing from other women in situations like hers.

Maybe it would all help Jake to understand.

It was the first time David had had the central role in anything, and he showed he was more than up to the challenge. The accumulation of acting experience came out, small facial gestures to indicate the weight of grief, the intensity of the physical confrontation (which also showed him to be a handy basketball player), a real depth of feeling. This was unlike any work he'd done before. He'd been given the chance to parade his talents, and he'd filled the role completely, making Jake into a rounded, tragic character.

Even when David had to emote on screen, something that might have seemed at odds with his acting style, he did it in a burst that grew more and more manic, which seemed perfectly in tune with the way he played Jake, becoming more and more unwrapped from the tightly wound character until all control was gone.

All put together, it showed just how much David had become an acting force to be reckoned with. And even he was pleased with his work on the pilot.

"I'm proud of it," he said. "It's where I really started to get some idea of how to do what I do."

It had been an education to make the show, but it had also been fun, since it teamed David with Billy Wirth, who'd been a close friend for several years—and, not surprisingly, a basketball buddy. Billy, too, had done an excellent job, but it was David's triumph.

And Zalman King's. He'd taken what could have been a very exploitative concept and made it into something more, something of substance, and quite touching. It resonated beyond tawdry erotica.

Certainly the people at Showtime thought so, for they bought an entire series. Which left David with a steady income and ongoing employment, as well as a part that he enjoyed, in a strange way, and understood.

"I'm the conduit through which America views the soft underbelly of women's erotic desires," he said wryly, adding, "Some say it's the part I was born to play."

Whether he was joking or expressing some hidden truth, it definitely altered his life. Being involved with a show that was specifically about sex didn't make him worry—and why should it? He hadn't been reluctant to let his own body be seen—and while the anthology pushed tenderly at the boundaries of soft-core pornography, it became regular viewing for quite a number of people, both women and men.

After the pilot, David had two minutes on each show to put himself across to an audience, to make them want to watch the episode that was about to start, and to tune in the next time. He'd developed his style over the last three years. Now he needed to focus it, to make it work for him in a different way. He needed to make himself intriguing. Knowing Jake's story, and being able to thrust himself into that background helped, but he needed to make an impact quickly, something that was both friendly and mysterious.

He worked on his facial expressions. They were subtle little moves, but they'd stand him in good stead for his later work. There was the Wounded Puppy Dog Face (known to X-Philes

David Duchovny at the 4th Annual Rock 'n'
Jock B-Ball Jam at Bren Event Stadium in
Irvine, California. *(Photo by Steve
Granitz/Retna Ltd.)*

David Duchovny and Gillian Anderson at the 52nd Annual Golden Globe Awards at the Beverly Hilton Hotel. *(Photo by Steve Granitz/Retna Ltd.)*

David Duchovny with Perrey Reeves at the premiere of *Batman Forever* at Mann's Village in Westwood, California. *(Photo by Steve Granitz/Retna Ltd.)*

David Duchovny at the 33rd N.A.T.P.E. Conference in Las Vegas. *(Photo by Joe Marzullo/Retna Ltd.)*

David Duchovny and a close friend. *(Photo by Guy Aroch/Retna Ltd.)*

On the set of "The X-Files" with David Duchovny.
(Photo by Guy Aroch/Retna Ltd.)

Dressed to investigate, David Duchovny (playing Fox Mulder) stares pensively at the camera. *(Photo by John Swannell/Camera Press/Retna Ltd.)*

David Duchovny at the 53rd Annual Golden Globe Awards at the Beverly Hilton Hotel. *(Photo by Sam Levi/Retna Ltd.)*

as WPDF), or the one that seemed to generate the best reaction—Vulnerable and Cute (V&C). By the time the series began filming, David had mastered them, and they made all the difference. He could still be his low-key self in front of the camera, but now there was so much more power in what he did.

He didn't go in to shoot every episode one by one. For the small amount of work involved, that would have been ridiculous. Instead, he filmed several at a time, and still does.

"I just do a minute at the beginning and in the end, six episodes in a day," he explained. "I call it my Jack Nicholson day because I figure I'm making Nicholson money for that day."

While David may make something much closer to Nicholson money now than when he started on "Red Shoe Diaries," these days his participation stems as much from personal satisfaction as from financial need. He *enjoys* playing Jake, and takes a slightly perverse pleasure in moving from Mulder, the international television heartthrob, to the man who's the confidant, but never the recipient, of female fantasies.

While critics had some reservations about the show—one called it "too studied to be erotic"—the general agreement was that "it looks like nothing else on TV." *Entertainment Weekly* went on to call a video anthology of episodes "erotically compelling stories," and a sexual undercurrent was present in every scene. But, for once, this was something that focused on women, not as objects, but as people, with lusts and desires of their own.

In some ways it was a short step from that to David's next movie, which also cast a close-up lens on women, this time as seen through the eyes of Henry Jaglom.

Venice/Venice referred to two cities with one name, in Italy and California. But, of course, there was far more to it than that.

In the film Jaglom was a movie director from Venice, California, attending the film festival in Venice, Italy, who became the object of a journalist's (Nelly Alard) affections.

She followed him back to America, where he was casting his new piece. There was no romance between them, no real conclusion to the story that had begun.

As with most Jaglom films, such as *New Year's Day*, it all revolved around conversation and ideas, in this case interviews with women who talked about the difference between romance on-screen and in real life.

While there was plenty to stimulate thought, as always in a Jaglom film, he remained the center of attention, the sun around which everyone else revolved, including, in small parts, David and Daphna Kastner (with whom David had co-starred in *Julia Has Two Lovers*).

It would have been easy to think that David's career had moved beyond this now, that he didn't need to be involved in another tight-budgeted independent movie that would never get beyond the art houses. But Jaglom had given him his first break, the springboard that had taken him to Hollywood and gotten him where he was now, just beginning to break out. More than that, David still had his intellectual roots, those mental ties to Princeton and Yale that revelled in ideas and theories, and things that weren't populist and mainstream. Being involved in *Venice/Venice* was more than paying back a debt; it was also a pleasure. And it made a complete, refreshing change from the work he'd become used to.

Not that he ended up with much to do. It was mostly women and Jaglom on camera, exploring what *People* called "Jaglom's deeply fissured, humorless psyche."

Still David had done his part, small though it was. Then his agent called. Would he be interested in trying out for a part opposite an up-and-coming actor named Brad Pitt?

SEVEN

Download: Dark Side

There was no doubt that David's landing a role in *Kalifornia* was the biggest thing that had happened to him in the industry so far. For the first time his talents would really be featured.

He'd still be playing second fiddle to one of Hollywood's rapidly up-and-coming couples, Brad Pitt and Juliette Lewis, but it was a strong part, with plenty of meat. And, more than that, even though he wasn't the lead, he was to be a hero of sorts.

For a short while, after *The Rapture* and *Beethoven*, it had looked as if David's career was really taking off. But then he'd reached a plateau of sorts. "The Red Shoe Diaries" kept him visible to a few people on cable television, but was unlikely to transform him into a star.

So this was another shot at the much-bigger time, one he wasn't about to—indeed, couldn't—pass up. After *A River Runs Through It*, Pitt was on his way to becoming one of the great movie heartthrobs of the nineties. To be in a movie with him, all the way through, not just for a few minutes, meant very high visibility. And that, finally, ought to lead somewhere. With some luck, this time the path would move rapidly upwards.

Stripped to its basics, *Kalifornia* was nothing more nor less than an old-fashioned morality tale in the guise of a road movie. Good became confused, went in search of something darker, found something evil, and eventually managed to conquer it. And when evil showed its face as a sociopathic serial killer, well, then you were talking about a subject that seemed to be very close to American hearts.

For whatever reason, the first half of the 1990s seemed to be the era of the serial killer in American cinema. The mass murderer was both glorified and vilified, and movies like *Natural Born Killers* not only generated a huge amount of press debate, but also plenty of dollars at the box offices and video stores around the country.

Kalifornia, with a screenplay by Tim Metcalfe from the story he wrote with Stephen Levy, was slightly ahead of the wave, a curious, shadowy mixture of film noir (about as American a movie genre as it was possible to find) and Quentin Tarantino-style gratuitous violence that struck an ambivalent note of emptiness.

But, although it had a decidedly offbeat edge, the presence of Pitt and Lewis meant it was destined for big billing. They'd been together as a couple for three years (having met when they worked together on a TV movie, "Too Young To Die") and wanted to work together. Undeniably, they both had plenty of talent and increasing appeal to a younger audience. In a movie that reflected the aimlessness of a "slacker" generation, the studios had a winner. At least, that was the theory.

David played Brian Kessler, a writer on the cusp between yuppie and hip, who lived in Philadelphia with his equally trendy girlfriend, a photographer called Carrie Laughlin (Michelle Forbes). He'd recently published a magazine article on serial killers, which he'd managed to parlay into a book contract. The only problem was, he had no real ideas for the book.

Until he visited the site of a serial killing.

With Carrie along to take pictures, it suddenly all came to life for him. Once they returned home, and he began to put his notes in order, inspiration struck. They'd head west, touring infamous murder sites. He'd write the text, and Carrie would take the pictures.

The journey would serve two purposes. It would provide material for the book, and it would also leave them in California, where Carrie wanted to live, a place, she felt, that might be more open to her work. They gave a ride to Early Grayce (Brad Pitt) and Adele Corners (Juliette Lewis).

Early and Adele were both hillbillies, living in a ratty trailer in a wrecking yard. She was a waitress, a childlike woman in both body and mind. He was an ex-con, on parole. And a very dangerous man.

Brian didn't know it yet, but he was about to get to know a real serial killer.

Killing was part of the natural order of things for Early. He didn't think twice about it, and it certainly didn't plague his conscience. As the trip progressed Brian fell under Early's spell. Adele snapped and allowed one of Early's victims to get away. That rebellion costs her her life. Brian knew he must confront Early to save his and Carrie's life.

Brian had refused to shoot a man once; this time the stakes were much higher. He crawled towards the gun that had been kicked out of his hand, and this time he pulled the trigger. Early fell back, blood gushing. Even then, he wasn't quite out. As Brian reached for the keys, a hand grabbed his arm. Without a qualm, he shot again, and Early was finally still.

The epilogue took place a few months later, on a grey November day. Waves dashed up to the beach house where Brian and Carrie were living. He was wrestling with the writing of his book, which had become the tale of Early Grayce, painful in his memory, but handed to him on a plate.

They were rebuilding their lives, slowly, gently. Carrie finally had a gallery that was interested in her work. Their lives were clearly divided into two parts, one marked "past," the other "future." And the future had begun. But it was bleaker and more weighted than they could ever have dreamed back in Philadelphia.

Kalifornia drew mixed reviews from the critics on its release, but it was really a much better movie than some were willing to admit. *Entertainment Weekly* didn't particularly like it, deeming it to be full of "ostentatious bad acting," a view endorsed by *The New York Times*, which said the film "lets its stars overact to the rafters as it vacillates between wild pretentiousness and occasional high style." Of course, the reviewer, Janet Maslin, also disparagingly called the film "baby noir" (mostly for the voice-overs by David), summing the whole thing up as "all attitude, and not much more."

New York, on first reading, seemed to leave the theater happy, admitting that "this arty movie is far from boring," and realizing that screenwriter Metcalfe "create[s] tensions among these four [characters] that become fascinating in a creepily erotic way." But at the final stroke, the critic decided that "*Kalifornia* wants to be a midnight-movie cult hit in the worst way; it about half makes it."

Variety at least, found something good in it, calling *Kalifornia* "an extremely handsome production imbued with a chilling surrealistic sensibility," adding that "When Brian cozies up to Early's easy machismo, his susceptibility and our own identification with the lure of danger are palpable and exciting." Here, finally, was the realization that it followed in the tradition of movies like Robert Mitchum's *The Night of the Hunter*, creating a "chilling core."

It was intended as a vehicle for Pitt and Lewis, and it was certainly the best work either of them had done to date. Pitt's portrayal of Early was nothing less than superb, always walking a knife-edge between the normal and the insane, while Lewis' little girl in a woman's body had an eerie, carnal quality about it.

While they were the ones who got to shine, David had a much harder role to play. For a start, arty yuppies ghoulishly touring murder sites didn't exactly engender audience sympathy. In the tradition of suspense movies, Brian Kessler was an ordinary man thrust into extraordinary circumstances where he finally had to prove himself. But, in a move away from that tradition, he wasn't a strong, upstanding fellow. He was weak, letting himself be lured deep into Early's web before being forced to extract himself. Nor was he "man enough" to protect his girlfriend.

As it turned out, David's heavy underplaying of Brian was just what the role needed. It was a case of less being more, as he hinted at the depths in his character, and allowed the audience to make him what they wanted. As *Variety* noted, all of the parts, in their own way, were "familiar caricatures." What became fascinating was the way "each breaks from the mold."

As Brian, David might not have come across as Mr. Popularity, but he was remarkably real. The vast majority of people aren't Cary Grant or Gary Cooper; they have their weaknesses and foibles. *That* was what David brought to the role. His stiff-lipped, slightly superior manner was able to put it across without words.

And while it was true, as *Entertainment Weekly* pointed out, that "Early and Brian [were] two men who wouldn't have four words to say to each other" they didn't become "brothers under the skin." Brian was a liberal, for better or worse, trying to let himself give others a chance. He and Early were opposite sides of the coin, even if it was the same coin. Brian could only kill when his life (and Carrie's) depended on it—and then only kill the person who was threatening them.

What glamour the role offered soon wore off. The trendy clothes, the vintage car—they all became irrelevant as the journey took place.

What David had to show was that the journey was as much inside Brian's head and heart as on the road.

And that he did in marvelous fashion. He accomplished it in small ways—a tighter look, a harsher tone. More than anything before, this looked like his big chance, and he wasn't about to let it slip away. Each move, the way each word was said, was carefully considered.

Given the script, there was no way he could hope to eclipse Brad Pitt in this "musical quartet" (as Pitt described it). But he more than held his own against someone who would become one of the screen's major stars in another year. He wasn't upstaged or out of his depth. He was a co-star, a second banana, and working within those limits, he did a superb job. You remembered him, and the look on his face as Brian killed Early, as much as you remembered Early himself.

The studio created plenty of hype about the picture; after all, Pitt and Lewis were both rising stars. For all the hype and the opening nationwide in the multiplexes, though, the film did nowhere near as well at the box office as everyone had hoped. The reviews didn't help, of course, but also the film was *too* dark, too ambivalent about its subject.

That was a shame, because audiences missed out on something worthwhile, a movie that was out of the ordinary, well-scripted and excellently acted (Michelle Forbes' portrayal of

Carrie was also well worth catching). Not to mention the fact that David had a brief nude scene—something that was becoming a relatively common occurence for him on the big screen, it seemed.

The visibility he enjoyed in *Kalifornia* gave David a lot of hope for the future. He was pleased with his work and with the finished product. It was as if he was gradually rising through the ranks, slowly but surely moving towards that starring role. The project had paid well. For once, he had a reasonable amount of money in his bank account, a pleasant change after a few years of struggling by on next to nothing. He knew that he had a real chance of becoming a star.

"You've got fifteen guys who are going to be the 'next big thing' and three of those guys are going to finish," he said. "I was making a living. It seemed like I would get my shot at some point."

He had what every artist, in any field, needs—the inner confidence that he'd eventually make it to the top. Without that, he'd have been sunk. Certainly, there were days when David was down and blue, when the parts he'd hoped for didn't come through, but that belief in himself didn't waver now, the way it had a few years earlier. He'd been through the wringer, he'd proved himself. The parts were finally getting bigger. It was only a matter of time . . .

He wanted success. David wasn't necessarily

bothered about all the trappings that came with it. He just needed to be able to stand on top of the mountain and understand that he'd arrived. Acting, and his career, was his focus. He didn't have the time to think about too much else. Since his move to Los Angeles, David had been adamant that he wanted to work in movies. That, he felt, was where his future lay. He didn't particularly enjoy television, even if it had been quite good to him. Most of the shows were second-rate, and even the better series quickly degenerated into drivel. Given a choice, he wanted to concentrate on films.

Of course, that hadn't stopped him doing either "Twin Peaks" or the "Red Shoe Diaries." But each was special; each had broken the TV mold, and, after the pilot, his involvement with "Red Shoe Diaries" was, at most, marginal. A couple of minutes per episode, regular money in the bank, well, that was hard to turn down. Of course, he hadn't refused advertising work either, having just completed a commercial for AT&T. But films, he truly felt, were what showed his real talents. And while he didn't know how, "I always had an abiding belief that things would work out for me."

So he remained set in his ideas, waiting and working for the break that would finally send him over the top. Since *Kalifornia* though, there'd been little of real value for him to read.

"And then my manager, who was agreeing with me in that I didn't want to do any television, sent me the script for "The X-Files" because she thought it was a really good script. She reads all the pilots, and that was the only one she sent me."

Because he had respect for her judgment, and because it was there, Duchovny looked at it, and agreed that it stood head and shoulders above most things on TV.

"I read it in my bathtub," he remembered, "and said, 'It's okay, it's a good pilot.'"

The writing was strong, the premise offbeat enough to appeal to him. And the character of Mulder suited him perfectly. It could almost have been written for him.

He was intrigued.

Every year, dozens of TV pilot shows are made. Every one is a gamble, a toss of the dice for something that might appeal, and be picked up to become a series. The odds are always against success. There's no formula for catching the public interest. Established stars bomb out as often as nobodies. It is, almost literally, a crap shoot.

David didn't believe that "The X-Files" stood a snowball's chance in hell of being picked up. All the things he liked about it stood in its way. It was quality work, rather than an attempt to pursue the lowest common denominator of entertainment. The weird premise was likely to be just too bizarre for Middle America. And so, naturally, he wanted to be involved.

The way he looked at it, shooting the pilot

would give him some satisfaction, a month in Vancouver, British Columbia (where the show was to be filmed), and a paycheck. That would be the end of it. "The X-Files" would never be heard of again, and he'd move on to his next film, with a little more experience and a little more money in his bank account.

There were only two problems. First, he had still to land the part. Second, he'd already committed to acting in a friend's movie—and he wasn't about to back out of that.

EIGHT

Open X-File:
PASSWORD PROTECTED

Still, when "The X-Files" creator Chris Carter asked him to audition for the role of Fox Mulder, David didn't back away. He didn't feel like he wanted the job, but who knew where it all might lead, somewhere down the road? He didn't even demur too much when he was asked to show up wearing a tie.

And it was the little pink pigs that really tipped the scales in his favor. Chris Carter is certain of that.

"I told him to wear a tie," Carter recalled. "He showed up in a tie with pink pigs all over it. I think that got him the job."

In truth, the final choice was between David and one other actor. While, as Carter noted, his rival's take on Mulder was "cooler, and a little more tortured," it was David's sense of irony (personified by the pink pigs) that swayed minds.

After that everything would have been perfect—except for the fact that David turned the job down. He'd already agreed to work on his friend's movie, and nothing was going to come in the way of that. The series' producers were dumbfounded. This simply wasn't the way actors behaved. They were convinced that David was the perfect person for the part, and this action only cemented the idea in their minds.

"It's the same with everything in life," David suggested, "relationships are unfortunately the same—if you don't need the other person then you're in the position of power. If you go into an audition and you don't really need the job, they're like, 'that guy's cool, there's something about him'—yeah, he wasn't kissing your ass."

And David certainly wasn't kissing any asses right now. It left Carter and the rest of the crew in a quandary. They wanted him, but he didn't seem especially interested. How could they get him to change his mind?

The answer was simple—and perhaps a perfect metaphor for the show they were going to work on. They applied pressure—"they just leaned on me," as David said.

But nothing seemed to work. Finally Randy Stone, the casting director, called David from

Vancouver, where they were getting ready to shoot the pilot, and told David that Chris Carter was willing to get on a plane and fly down to see him.

That did the trick.

"I was just such a pushover that just those words, that he would fly, that did it."

And the fact that Stone offered him a raise from his original fee didn't hurt matters, either.

David was in, and during March 1993 he headed north to Vancouver, Canada, ready to shoot the pilot for "The X-Files."

What he didn't know at the time was that his co-star, Gillian Anderson, had been awarded her role as Mulder's partner, Agent Dana Scully, by the skin of her teeth.

Carter's insistence that the characters— especially Scully's—"had to be real" precluded finding some glamorous, gorgeous model-type for the part. Scully was a no-nonsense professional in the mold of Clarice Starling, Jodie Foster's award-winning FBI role in *The Silence of the Lambs*. He wanted someone who looked as if she could use her brain more than her body.

Gillian was a theater actress, with only one television appearance, a guest role on "Class of '96" to her credit. Like David, she wasn't too fond of television as a medium, and only ended up auditioning for Scully out of financial necessity. It might have been the best move she ever made.

"When she came into the room," Carter said

later, "I just knew she was Scully. I just felt it . . . She had an intensity about her; intensity always translates across the screen."

Carter might have been convinced, but Fox, who were bankrolling everything, remained skeptical. Gillian was brought back for another audition. Time was running out. Filming was due to begin in a matter of weeks. A decision had to be made. Finally Carter just told the people from Fox, " 'Look, this is the person I want. This is Dana Scully.' And everybody looked at me and said, 'Okay.' "

One thing Carter adamantly didn't want was any kind of romance between Mulder and Scully. They were meant to be professional people, investigating serious, if weird, cases. That would be the focus of the show.

"It's not going to be 'Moonlighting,' " insisted Bob Greenblatt, a Vice President at Fox. But there were still plenty at the network who wanted sexual tension and a relationship that went beyond work for the two characters; they felt it would help the ratings. Indeed, a press release by Fox's PR department before the show first aired described Mulder and Scully's relationship as becoming "more complex with each case, slowly emerging as a heady mix of professional competitiveness, witty repartee, and a mutual attraction that is heightened by the intensity of their tasks and the close proximity in which they work."

* * *

As it was, the shooting of the pilot began later than was originally scheduled, partly because of the problems Carter had had in getting Fox to accept Gillian, and also because of the number of pilots shooting in Vancouver, which meant difficulties in finding people to fill the necessary technical positions.

David and Gillian barely had time to become acquainted before filming began. In fact, the only rehearsal they were able to squeeze in was a table reading—sitting around a table and reading the lines—rather than on the set.

"I was totally loose," David said of their first rehearsal scene together, when Scully had been assigned to work with Mulder and the X-Files. "This was *my* room, these were *my* people. . . . I wish I'd been that good when the cameras were rolling. So I played the scene in a kind of sarcastic way . . . and Gillian was just completely thrown by it . . . she was shocked that anybody would talk to her that way. That's exactly how she should have reacted. It was perfect." And it created an immediate rapport between the two, which was an absolute necessity if the show was to have any chance of success.

Filming lasted for two weeks, much of it in grey, rainy weather—typical for the Northwest, but which also set a dark, eerie mood for the show. All done, the cast went their separate ways and waited to hear the verdict from the network.

David returned to L.A. to try and find another movie, something that might capitalize on the notices he received for *Kalifornia*. Instead he found a girlfriend.

He'd dated, of course—who was going to turn down an invitation from someone like him—but the real relationships in his life had been few and far between. And, coming off "The X-Files" pilot, eager to move his career ahead, looking for one was the last thing on his mind. Which was why he found one, of course.

His bank account might not have been exactly bulging, but after the pilot there was a little money to spare. He could afford to treat himself to a new suit, a luxury he hadn't been able to afford in a while.

But shopping at Fred Segal's department store in Santa Monica, in May 1993, he just couldn't decide. Both the grey and the blue fit well. They both looked good. David couldn't choose between them, trying them on, checking himself in the mirror, taking them off. Finally he did the only thing that sprang to mind—he asked someone else.

She was one aisle over, in the women's section, shopping for lingerie with her mother when he asked her opinion. It could have seemed like a pickup line, but David appeared so sincere. He honestly couldn't make up his mind.

The young woman looked at the suits, felt the material, studied the cut. Get them both, she advised finally. David did. And after he'd made his purchase, they began to talk.

Her name was Perrey Reeves. She was twenty-two, a full decade younger than David. But that age difference didn't matter. He was struck by her looks and her manner. And she was equally taken with him, his reserve, his way of considering words before he spoke, of being so exact.

Like half the people around Los Angeles, she was an actress. So far, though, her credits had been so limited as to be almost non-existent. To her, David was a success story already. Never mind the fact that he wasn't a star. He'd worked often; he was supporting himself by acting. That was success enough to her.

Right from that first meeting in Fred Segal's they knew there was a connection between them. Something just clicked. It felt *right*, as if it was meant to be. Beginning that night, David and Perrey saw each other often.

The executives at Fox sat down to watch "The X-Files" pilot in late May, after Carter and his technical team had completed their post-production work.

"It screened gangbusters," said Sandy Grush-ow, who headed up Fox's Entertainment Group. Even top people in the company, like Rupert Murdoch and chairman Lucie Salhany, voiced their approval.

"The X-Files" was on the fall schedule.

Even though David had originally believed that "UFOs would get boring after three or four episodes," he rapidly became one of the show's biggest boosters. Fox had picked up "The X-Files," but they were treating it like an awful stepchild, something they were saddled with but didn't really want. Their attitude, David said, was as if they thought, "And oh yeah, there's this other little show called 'The X-Files.'"

The show going into production signalled major changes in David's life. Since the series would continue to shoot in Vancouver, that meant the great upheaval of moving there. He may still not have believed that he'd be employed for a full season, let alone beyond that, but the hectic filming schedule meant that he had to find somewhere to live up there.

He didn't keep his apartment in Los Angeles. It was time for a change, to let the nomadic side of his personality rise again. But it did mean he'd have to leave Perrey, just as their relationship was beginning to take off. It was hard, but they agreed to see each other whenever they could—he'd fly down when he had a break, or she'd fly up for the weekend when time allowed. To most people it wouldn't have seemed the most satisfactory way to carry on, but David had never claimed to be cut from the ordinary mold, and, he admitted, if he'd stayed in L.A. he might not have spent a greater amount of time with her, anyway.

But stuck in his Vancouver sublet, he had to wonder if he'd done the right thing. Everything that was familiar was now more than a thousand miles away down the coast. The new apartment was barren, even though he was settled in. No pictures on the walls, nothing to give away any traces of his personality. He was here to work, not to carve out a life for himself. David still believed it would be only temporary, nothing more than an interruption of real life.

And work he certainly did. Along with Gillian, he was thrown into the ring as they spent anywhere from twelve to sixteen gruelling hours a day, five days a week, on the set or on location. Much of it was outside (wherever the episode is set, all the filming is done in and around Vancouver), in rain, wind, whatever the elements could throw at them.

It was a challenge, both physically and mentally. David was no stranger to the pressure and intensity of acting, but this was different from anything he'd ever known. From the moment he began work on the series proper, all the old rules stopped applying.

Making a movie was hard work—early calls, long days, brief periods on camera followed by long spaces of doing nothing. But it was finite. After six weeks or so, it was over, and everyone had time to regroup before moving on to the next project. A television series shared some of those elements, mostly the long days, but there was never any let up. As soon as one show was wrapped, actors and crew moved straight on to the next one. There was no time to decompress and really become a human being again. It was like running endless marathons back-to-back.

"I had never experienced that kind of load," David admitted. "There were many days the first year when I would just go home and think, 'I can't do it. I can't go back to work anymore.'"

It didn't help that as the cast and crew toiled through the summer, they were working in a vacuum. The executives at Fox were pleased with what they were seeing, but who knew how well it would play to a prime-time audience?

As September arrived, they were going to find out.

Before the pilot aired as the show's premiere, though, things didn't look too good. In its round-up of the new fall shows, *Entertainment Weekly* announced, "We know—this show's a goner," which didn't seem to bode too well for the future.

On Friday, September 10, 1993, America had a chance to judge for itself. Though the show hadn't been heavily promoted, it still garnered a Nielsen rating of 7.9 and 15 percent of the viewing audience. That was more than encouraging—it was a cause for celebration.

But that could only be brief. On Monday it was back to the grindstone, relieved and a little more secure, knowing that out there at least *someone* cared.

So who, exactly, was this Fox Mulder character that David had signed on to play? He was an FBI agent, who, at his own request, had undertaken the task no one else wanted—investigating the mysterious X-Files, the incidents that seemed to defy rational explanation. His obsession with them had earned him the nickname "Spooky" from his colleagues, a handle he both liked and hated.

A brilliant man, he'd attended Oxford University in England, earning a degree in psychology before joining the FBI, and graduating high in his class from the Training Academy at Quantico. No sooner had he become an agent, assigned to the Behavioral Science Unit of the Violent Crimes Section, than he wrote a psychological profile of a wanted serial killer, which led to the quick arrest of Monty Props. The profile was so accurate and detailed that it became part of the curriculum of Quantico.

He'd also published a monograph in 1988, "On Serial Killers and the Occult," which won him some distinction (and helped earn him that nickname).

But it was the X-Files that were really calling Mulder, and in 1991 he finally persuaded his bosses to let him work on them. In his past—in his own family—Fox had an X-File of his own. When he was thirteen, his sister Samantha, then nine years old, vanished. While it was never proven, and probably could *never* be proven, Mulder knew in his heart that she'd been abducted by aliens, and his memories of the event somehow altered. He'd even undergone regression therapy in 1989 in an attempt to uncover the truth in his head.

Samantha's disappearance tore the family apart. Fox's father, then a high-ranking official at the State Department, pulled strings, but a thorough investigation could find no leads. Eventually his parents divorced.

Fox's great mission in life, the thing that kept him going, kept him dedicated even when the pressure was on to close the X-Files altogether, was to find his sister.

The problem with Mulder was that he was too good at his job. He began to find answers to these old incidents, and some of them hinted strongly at conspiracies of silence and disinformation at the highest levels of government. For that information to leak out to the general public, letting them know their officials in Washington couldn't be trusted, was simply intolerable.

So a spy needed to be installed. Agent Dana Scully had recently graduated from Quantico. She had a bachelor's degree in physics, and had then completed her M.D. before joining the Bureau. She was the one sent to work with Mulder, and to report back on his investigations and findings, to keep tabs on him and make sure he didn't get out of hand.

With her strong scientific background, she would also act as a foil to Mulder's wilder ideas. He might have had a poster reading "I Want To Believe" on his office wall, but Scully was one who could be trusted to look for the rational explanation.

Going into the series, that was how the back story stood. Motives and characters had been established and rounded out. The numbers for the premiere had been strong, and that trend continued for a few weeks.

However, they began to tail off as fall progressed, then rising again at the beginning of 1994, and continued to rise throughout the rest of the season. The finale grabbed an 8.8 rating—the best numbers "The X-Files" had managed so far.

By then the show had definitely acquired an identity of its own, and its stars, especially David, were rapidly developing followings. He might not have been too widely noticed during his film appearances, but people were certainly beginning to make up for that now.

There was something very alluring about his enigmatic personality. Yes, he was handsome, almost always immaculate in his suit, very clean-cut, and athletic. But there was much, much more, depths that were only hinted at, places of shadow and darkness that Mulder deliberately kept hidden.

David's minimalist style was able to put that across. He was an actor who never revealed too much; quite the opposite, really. David had, as Chris Carter pointed out, "A clear, quick mind, an intelligence beyond book smarts, and a tremendous amount of personal magnetism."

High praise indeed. But while viewers in general were more than happy to react to Mulder on an intellectual level, David's problem, he said jokingly, was that, "I'm trying desperately to get people to appreciate me as a sex symbol."

It wasn't something he really needed to worry about. The show hadn't been on the air too long before the first stirrings of interest in David began—quite appropriately, given the focus of the show, on the Internet.

"I think it's great that people like the show," David said, "I'm flattered that people like it and my character." Still, he added, "I really don't think about it all that much."

One person who knew all too well how sexy he could be was Perrey Reeves. Despite the distance, they were still together, and, said David, "We see each other every other weekend." She'd pack a bag and fly north for two days to be with him.

It was hard on them both, but they knew what the business was like—you had to go where the work was. You had to pursue success. Otherwise you might as well go off and do something else, get a regular job and put all the dreams behind you. And right now he was the one who seemed to have a real shot at the big time. Although whether it would last beyond the first season would remain a question mark for a while longer yet.

So they took their time together as they could, and valued it. But when she left on a Monday morning, David's loneliness would return. He might have seemed like a person content to be alone, his emotions almost hermetically sealed, but that was just a facade. He needed company. And what could be better company than a dog, man's best friend?

Blue, the animal he adopted, was part border collie, part terrier, a long-haired animal who'd accompany him to the set, on location—everywhere. Named for the Bob Dylan song, "Tangled Up in Blue," the dog was exactly what he needed.

"The idea was that she would help me with my blues," he explained to *TV Guide.* "training her is like training for being a dad . . . I've got a dog staring at me every morning saying, 'Let's go play Frisbee.' And I have to say, 'Don't you know how hard Daddy works?'"

Blue certainly did help with his blues, becoming quite a favorite of everyone on the set, and being treated just as if she was another member of the crew (and she actually became a member of the cast for the episode "Ice").

Something else that must have helped David's spirits were the reviews of the show that began to appear. After initially dismissing it, the critics had finally begun to notice "The

X-Files," and had realized that was not another run-of-the-mill show. It wasn't doing particularly well in the ratings—it would finish 113th out of 132 shows broadcast in prime time—but one way and another the word was gradually leaking out.

In an about-face from its original viewpoint, *Entertainment Weekly* announced, "I'm hooked on 'The X-Files,'" adding that it was "the most paranoid, subversive show on TV right now . . . There's marvelous tension between Anderson . . . and Duchovny, who has the haunted, imploring look of a true believer."

And while *People* pitched Mulder into the same camp as Twin Peaks' Agent Cooper, the writer did admit, "If the producers can keep the mood spooky, this show will have its devoted adherents."

As the first season progressed, and 1993 turned into 1994, *Entertainment Weekly*, as if to finish penance for its original prognosis, ran a short article about the show, pointing out that it had "no high-minded moral to teach, no winking irony to impart; all it wants to do is shake your faith in reality," before concluding, "the series gives off a warm glow of assured wit. Give yourself over to 'The X-Files' and you'll be in the hands of people who know exactly how to mess with your mind."

USA Today struck quite bluntly to the point— "File this under your 'must-see' heading: 'The

X-Files' just keeps getting better. And weirder. And scarier."

There was no doubt that the show was pushing the limits further and further each week. But it wasn't UFOs and aliens each time. The bizarre could also be on earth, and the way some truths were officially covered up was every bit as spooky and scary as any case the agents were called to investigate.

The poster in Mulder's office said that he wanted to believe. That was fine, and perfectly understandable—belief offered him an explanation for his sister's disappearance. But what about David? Did he mirror his character in that way? Or had the rationalism of years spent studying and analyzing removed the idea of taking things on faith?

Neither and both, really. He walked the fine line between belief and skepticism, telling *TV Guide*, "There may be something out there. . . . If I were to bet, I would say that it is more likely than not that there are other life forms." And he elaborated on that in *People*.

"I believe in the possibility that there are other forms of life. But as it gets played out on the show, well, it's hard for me to believe that there's actually a liver-eating serial killer."

But while he was willing to define himself as "a skeptic of specifics," David did admit to one curious encounter.

"I was in Ocean City, Maryland, in 1987. I

looked up and saw something that looked like a plane. I looked away for a second and it was gone. It was low and big. I couldn't believe my eyes. I just glanced away for a second and when I looked back it was gone."

Obviously, the incident had stayed with him, and preyed on his thoughts from time to time, especially since beginning work on "The X-Files."

Curiously, while David was willing to voice his doubts about the strange, rather than plunge into wholehearted acceptance like Mulder, Gillian Anderson, who provided the cool voice of reason as Scully, was a confirmed believer, who had "always had a basic belief in the paranormal."

David had obviously thought long and hard about the supernormal appeal of the show, however—the graduate student in him wouldn't ever lie down and rest completely—and formulated a theory about its attraction, and the way many viewers so desperately wanted to believe its idea of other existences, of aliens, of humans with strange powers that defied explanation.

"It's a New Age show, definitely," he told *Playboy*. "It's a secular religious show. It's saying that miracles do happen. Critics have said that the show is dark, but it's actually light—not in tone or execution but in philosophy. Most TV shows depict the world as being extremely dangerous. 'The X-Files' ushers you into a world of latter-day saints where we can still have magic. The time of miracles has not passed, it says. We're living in it."

"The X-Files" tapped into a vein. Or, perhaps, two veins that joined at some point. The first was, as David said, very much of the "New Age"—with people wanting more spiritually, whether it be a belief in the power of crystals, angels as popular symbols, an explanation of crop circles, past-life regression, or anything else. There was a need to believe, and the show went some way towards feeding that hunger, or at least letting people feel they weren't alone with their appetites.

The other vein was darker, and considerably more wordly. Since Watergate brought down a President, people's trust in their leaders had gradually been declining. As files were made public, it had become quite obvious that different governments, and governing bodies, all over the world, had covered up any number of potentially embarrassing incidents. There was plenty of evidence to hint at large global conspiracies, even, possibly, a massive attempt to protect the real assassins of John F. Kennedy in 1963. "The X-Files" played on those theories, too, with great regularity, fueling ideas of paranoia almost every week, something David readily acknowledged.

"If you look at the people in the militia groups and the conspiracies they believe, we kind of traffic in that," he said. "I think the show is simply of our time. I don't believe that art creates what happens in life. They are definitely connected, just not causally. There are literal-minded folks who say, 'You know, ever since *Jurassic Park* came out, people have been getting killed by dinosaurs, and it's Steven Spielberg's fault.' To me, that kind of connection never makes much sense. The people who advocate thought police have always been with us. They date as far back as Plato. . . . It's always scary to see who you really are. People are trying to ascribe blame—'If you hadn't made 'The X-Files,' the world would be a better place.' I'm not saying the world's a better or worse place because of the show. I'm just saying that it's a little more crowded."

It was, at the end of the day, simply entertainment. What "The X-Files" offered to America on a Friday night was an hour of escapism, an intelligently scripted, well-acted, and thoughtfully produced way of passing the time with a television. David had very definite thoughts on what made the show special.

"It's intelligent writing for television and there's nothing like it," he explained. "In fact, I don't think there's ever been anything like it on TV because all the scary shows have been kind of stupid. 'The Twilight Zone' is interesting, but it's goofy, campy. 'Outer Limits' is campy. I don't think we're campy. We're conceived of as an actual drama rather than some kitschy slice of Americana from this day and age. I mean, we may turn into that, I can't say, but I just don't think there's anything like it right now."

However, the bottom line was that people would see what they wanted to see in the show, as director-producer Rob Bowman explained.

"I'm fascinated by what [some people] read into it," he said. "We don't have time to put in everything they think they see."

And given that some of the scripts have been written in three days, it's impossible not to believe him.

Although the first season's rankings weren't as high as Fox would have liked, it was still renewed for a second season. Fox needed quality programming. "The X-Files" certainly qualified on that score—and the show had found an audience among the magic demographic everybody wanted to reach, the 18–34 year olds. The mixture of science fiction, horror, cover-ups and comradeship was exactly what they were after, combining high-tech and distant belief.

The audience tended to be educated, upscale, and—most significantly—computer-literate. "The X-Files" quickly became an on-line hit, with David as the first on-line heartthrob, as women (and some men) banded together in the David Duchovny Estrogen Brigade, an unofficial fan club which clogged cyberspace after each new episode to discuss the nuances of his performance, and, not incidentally, his body.

America Online developed an X-Files folder, to be followed by others, until there were over one hundred "X-Files" sites on the Net.

"It definitely was one of those wonderful coincidences," Chris Carter explained. " 'The X-Files' and the Internet on-line services sort of came of age at the same time and so here you've got an audience which is computer literate and capable and they happen to watch 'The X-Files.' It was one of those things where—there's probably a really pithy way to say this—the medium and the audience all found their way to one another."

But while Carter was happy to court the on-line crowd, making frequent conference appearances on Delphi and CompuServe, David didn't pay much attention to it. During the season he was far too busy, with workdays that seemed endless, followed by weekends devoted to rest or visits from Perrey.

By the time the first season of "The X-Files" was over, the last thing he wanted was to be delving around, seeing what fans had written about him. He needed a break from Mulder.

The time off was both good and bad. He left Vancouver, ten months after arriving, with a signed contract for another season, which meant he wouldn't have to look for employment anytime soon. Money had stopped being a problem. He'd become a recognizable face, even if it was for doing something he'd never really expected to do. And, while he was enjoying his time off, reruns of the show were gathering a larger audience for next year.

The downside was that back in Los Angeles, he realized he'd become a person without a real home.

"I didn't have a life in Vancouver," he said, "and I fantasized I had a life here. Now I realize I don't have a life anywhere." The intensity of production, the endless grind of working, had made him into someone who was purely an actor, as opposed to a whole person.

"But now," he continued, "when I'm faced with myself as a person, I'm unrecognizable to myself. I lost the skill of talking about how I feel, except for stupid actor-needs."

If not for the presence of Perrey, Los Angeles would be a total disappointment to him. At least he had the opportunity to spend time with her when he wasn't exhausted, to slowly discover himself again, and recharge his batteries as the time for heading back north slowly rolled around again.

It was impossible not to think ahead to that, and to the problems that would be coming. Gillian Anderson had announced that she was pregnant, having married one of the crew members. Rumors had circulated that she'd be replaced, but in the end the producers had stuck by her. Still, it meant shooting around her, arranging special angles for shots, making sure she wasn't too tired.

David had been the first to know; the trust

between them had grown as the season of filming dragged on. But when they returned the pressure on him would be greater than ever, as she'd be able to do less and less.

But he tried, as much as possible, to put it all from his mind and be happy in the here and now. He had Perrey, and his yoga—something he'd discovered after first moving to California—to keep him centered. This was a vacation, after all, to be enjoyed.

The only problem was that it was too short. Just around the time he truly began to feel relaxed it was time to return to Vancouver.

NINE

Press Return
to Continue

The first season had been arduous and draining for everyone concerned with the show. The second wouldn't be any better, but they were all prepared for it now, ready to pace themselves over the long days—and nights—and it showed.

With the renewal, the writers felt a greater confidence, which showed in the scripts. Scully, and particularly Mulder, were given freer rein to show their personalities.

And that meant making "The X-Files" more slyly humorous.

It had been there, to a small degree, in the earlier shows. But everyone had been more concerned with the idea being taken seriously. Now they were established, and they were in a position to push the envelope a bit.

David had always been very intent on his acting, perfecting that minimalist style which was so suited to Fox Mulder. Under the deadpan expression, though, he was actually a very funny person, with a quip or a practical joke to lighten the mood. He was the one who would stick his head through the fronds of a fern and perform his Arte Johnson impersonation, or spray Gillian with white rice during an episode dealing with maggots.

His humor could take some strange turns, too, as in the episode where Mulder went swimming, emerging from the pool in tiny red Speedo briefs.

"Oh, that was completely gratuitous," he admitted. "You rarely see a man wearing a Speedo on television, unless he's ['Baywatch' star] David Hasselhoff. I thought it would be funny, since Agent Mulder ordinarily has a suit practically tattooed on him."

Funny, yes. But it also served to stir hormones across the land and cause people, especially women, to burn up the Internet wires discussing it, and view the scene over and over in slow-motion in an attempt to discover whether he "dressed" to the left or right. And to David, that was hilarious.

During the first season he'd been "occasionally kind of happy with my work." Mulder had still been somewhat undefined as a character. By the time he was working again, that had changed. "The X-Files" was going to be around for a while, and David had a chance to make a real contribution, to give Mulder some history and solidity. And, "it was important for me as an actor to make that history as interesting as I could."

That desire resulted in David returning to writing. Not poetry this time, but the drama he'd abandoned after graduate school.

An idea came to him after reading an article in *The New Yorker* about the "racial purity" policies that Spain's General Franco had wanted to implement. From there his mind took a short step to immigration into the United States and the *alien* immigration. He took the story to Carter, who loved it, and worked up the script.

"David has a terrific story sense," Carter said. "He has good ideas. It's a nice way to hang out and spend time together and the show has benefitted."

The episode David came up with, "Colony," didn't really stray too far from the territory "The X-Files" had established as its own, dealing with aliens and a killer with the ability to morph (change shapes) who had been sent after them. But it also trod on some very personal Mulder ground.

Called to his father's home on Martha's Vineyard, Mulder discovered the family assembled—the full family, including his long-lost sister, Samantha, back after vanishing twenty-two years before, and the adopted daughter of one of the aliens.

"Colony" and "End Game," the episode which finished the story the following week, gave a great deal of insight into Mulder, the relationships in his family, his motivation for being involved with the X-Files, and his unresolved love for his sister. It also marked a turning point in the friendship between Mulder and Scully. In the past, Mulder's watchwords had been to trust no one. Where Samantha was concerned, however, he was willing to trust everyone and anyone who might have information about her. Lying in his hospital bed, recovering from hypothermia, he realized that finding Samantha had been a very personal, private obsession, one he'd detailed to nobody. Finally he was willing to open up a little, and let down his guard enough to tell Scully. Until then they'd been colleagues. Close ones, perhaps, with bonds forged in adversity at work, but now he'd opened the door and let her into his life. Only a little, but it meant a lot.

And, as David said, "Colony" and "End Game" together "created a unique mythology for television in the character, and I'm really proud of that fact—that I was conscious enough to say to Chris, 'Look, I have some ideas, I want to be involved with the creation of this myth.' "

Writing gave David an even greater involvement in the series, and took up some of that valuable free time which he never seemed to have enough of. It also increased his already vested interest in the show being successful—he had a bigger stake in it now. But success wasn't enough. He wanted, just as he had at the start of his acting career, to be involved with a quality product. And, in the 1994–95 season, he honestly believed he was, saying "we really became the best show on television."

David was involved in the writing of one more episode during the season, the finale, "Anasazi," whose climax was extended through the first *two* episodes of the third season. It was probably no real coninicidence that the story David chose to tell further illuminated the Mulder family (indeed, it included the murder of Mulder's father), sketching the involvement of Bill Mulder in secret alien experimentation, and throwing a few more rays of light on the alien abduction of Samantha that Fox had always believed in.

It showed that David had given a lot of thought to his character. Not only how to portray him on-screen, but also what made him tick, his quirks, his passions. He wasn't content to show up on the set, say his lines, and collect his paycheck every week. Mulder, and "The X-Files," meant more to him than that. He wrote because it helped him understand the character, to fill in the blank spaces that surrounded him, and it made him more real and tangible in David's mind.

Of course, Mulder was all too real to David anyway—he was living the part eighty hours a week, just as he had the year before. Gillian, too, was continuing to carry a heavy workload all through her pregnancy, stopping only a week before she gave birth to her daughter, Piper, then returning to the set in a matter of days.

Everyone had been prepared for her to take time off, her absence being explained by a supposedly-alien abduction—although the third season would show that it was actually more down to earth than that—reminiscent of Samantha Mulder's.

In the real world, David only had to perform one episode without his screen partner. But it did have a few compensations; he was able to act with his off-screen partner, Perrey. In a show titled "3," she played Kristen Kilar, a woman who spent her free time with vampires, and eventually became one of them.

What made this particular episode so remarkable was that it was the only time that Mulder let another, all too human, facet of his character show—he and Kristen slept together. Art imitating life.

Having Perrey there, having to act making love to his real-life lover, was hard for David, as he told *TV Guide*.

"The only time I was really scared was when I had to act with my girlfriend. To show different sides of yourself, to be more honest—*that* was scary."

Perrey also provided some light relief in an "X-Files" world that was putting more and more pressure on David. He knew, with Gillian's condition, that he'd have to really carry the weight for the season. But he held up remarkably well, and much of that was due to Perrey. She was in Vancouver as often as she could manage, giving him emotional support.

In the rare times he wasn't working, they could be together at the apartment he'd sublet on Point Grey, overlooking the water. Both were vegetarians and practitioners of yoga. In the increasing hubbub of the world around him, David needed a center, and Perrey helped provide that. She'd affixed a series of Post-it notes to his refrigerator, each containing one of Deepak Chopra's tips for attaining the fountain of youth. And, not quite as an afterthought, she'd added one more—"Think about Perrey"—which, David joked, he didn't think would help him stay young.

He'd finally got around to decorating the apartment, although, as might have been expected, it was in a fairly minimalist style. There was some Shaker furniture, its lines simple and clean, a few posters from 1950s movies on the walls, and above the bed a stylized Inuit drawing of a hummingbird—a very Northwest addition to the room. Overall the place seemed sparse and withdrawn, the home of someone who was rarely there, either physically or mentally.

Although his schedule continued to be gruelling, David was becoming used to it. And from the beginning of the season, it was obvious that all the work was going to pay off. The ratings were consistently higher than the year before, and Fox started to put some promotional muscle behind the show.

It certainly didn't hurt the series—or David, for that matter—when awards nominations began to pour in. During its first year, "The X-Files" had taken two Emmys, for its title sequence and theme music, as well as several others for writing. But now the big guns were beginning to weigh in. David found himself nominated for a Viewers for Quality Television Award as best actor in a drama series (Gillian was nominated for best actress). The Television Critics' Association nominated the show as both best drama series and program of the year. This time around it was nominated in seven different Emmy categories, including outstanding drama series. And, perhaps best of all, "The X-Files" took the Golden Globe award as best dramatic series. It was a wonderful harvest for something that nobody had expected to succeed.

"The X-Files" had really arrived. And Fox realized it. To push viewing figures even higher, towards the end of the season they offered a one-hour introduction to the show, its characters and conspiracies, and some highlights of the action.

It was a wonderful idea. Many who were interested in watching, or who had begun, were confused by some of the mysterious people who flitted in and out, like X or the Cigarette-Smoking Man, pulling strings behind the scenes. This primer gave them a chance to discover precisely what they'd been missing.

Plenty of people took advantage of the opportunity, then kept watching the show. "Anasazi," the cliffhanger which ended the second season, leaving Mulder for dead in a buried railroad car, had a Nielsen rating of 9.6 (as opposed to 8.3 for "The Erlenmeyer Flask," which closed the first season). Several times the ratings had risen above 10.00, even though the network kept switching it around on the schedule—from Friday to Sunday, then back to Friday. At the end of its second year, "The X-Files" was ranked 62nd out of 142 programs—a huge improvement. For many people it had hit that designation known as "appointment television"—a show that was either watched every single week or taped by its viewers. And given that most of the viewers were in the ultra-desirable 18–34 age range, educated, and upwardly mobile, it was in a very strong position.

The increased visibility of the series had also

served to make David a very public figure, a true nighttime heartthrob. The buzz about him had spread from the Internet into magazines and newspapers. Suddenly everyone from *Cosmopolitan* to *Playboy* wanted an interview with him, to know his history and his views on everything under the sun. He'd achieved in television what he'd set out to do in films— he'd become a star.

Even famous people wanted to meet him.

"A production assistant came up behind me," he related to *TV Guide*, "and said, 'Robin Williams would like to meet you, David.' And as I was turning, I said, 'No, he wouldn't.' And he was *standing right there.* And he goes, 'Oh, yes, he would!' So that was kind of funny."

What he found, though, like many others before him, was that fame wasn't quite all it was cracked up to be.

"Celebrity's no fun," he said. "There's really nothing nice about it. Celebrity is being known. It's no fun to be known. I imagine it's fun to be known for something good that you did, or for something noteworthy, but unfortunately the kind of celebrity television brings is monochromatic."

Partly it was because he could no longer have a life to call his own. Now that his face was public property, whenever he was out, trying to live his life normally, he was stared at, watched, scrutinized. Knowing that people were always looking at him stopped him from being spontaneous, or silly, or just being himself. It imposed constraints on him. More than that, though, it made it harder for David to research his craft.

"I fear that people will get to know me," he told *Playboy*. "You see that guy sitting over there? When you become a celebrity, it's harder to walk into a room and observe that man— maybe rip off a move or gesture and use it later. All of a sudden that man looks at me and thinks, Oh, it's that famous guy, and then he's not himself anymore. He's suddenly the performer. He's acting. That's death for me."

It was something he'd obviously considered and analyzed. David, who'd always been the outsider growing up, the observer, was still the outsider, by dint of his new celebrity, but he'd become the observed. The lack of anonymity restricted him.

Unlike a movie actor, who becomes known over the course of several roles, the television star is associated with one part, the one that made him or her into a household name, be it large or small. To people in America, and now all over the world, David was Fox Mulder. The roles he'd had before were irrelevant. He'd brought Mulder to life, and so he *was* Mulder.

It might be a cause for worry, but those thoughts could be postponed for later. The show was still only in its second season. In time the association of David and Mulder could well become indelible. For now, burgeoning stardom and all, there was still a season to be completed, which meant that David could turn his back on the reporters for a while and focus on his real love—acting.

The increased confidence among everyone involved on "The X-Files" glittered all through the second season. The stories were stronger. They took more chances. With Gillian back and fit (she brought her daughter to the set, with a nanny to help her cope with the double work-load), things were running smoothly again. The sly repartee between Mulder and Scully was turned up a notch, the humor drier and more prevalent than before. This was a show that had found its feet and wasn't afraid to show it. It was quality television, something anyone would be proud to be associated with. The writing struck a fine balance between the intellect and dramatic sense. It went where no one had gone before, but it wasn't the son of "Star Trek," by any means. It wasn't even science fiction. Thanks to the tightly focused vision of Chris Carter, who remained firmly in overall control, and to the acting of David and Gillian, "The X-Files" had developed its own identity.

The second season was a lesson in television, how to sustain excellence week after week. Unlike most series, "The X-Files" gave its main characters a chance to stretch themselves, to show their talents.

For David, that meant constantly striving to achieve something, and not always succeeding.

That was fine; the journey to reach the goal was sometimes more important than the goal itself.

"The best actors convey the idea that they never truly get there," he said. "The viewer senses failure and disappointment from them. I love when you can smell failure in an actor's performance, because acting is about displaying yourself for money and for people you don't know. There is a great cost to your personal life. . . . The best actors have an air of failure even at the height of their success."

Mulder, of course, had his successes, but in the larger picture—uncovering the big truth that was out there—he could never win. The odds, not to mention the power and the influence, were all stacked against him.

But that was part of what made his character so appealing. He was a decent guy trying his damnedest to fight corruption, to take on the giant. It was a story with so many precedents— David and Goliath, Don Quixote, *Mr. Smith Goes to Washington*, even Woodward and Bernstein uncovering the Watergate scandal and eventually toppling a government. The odds were appalling, but on occasion the little guy could make a big change.

The fact that Mulder had a very personal stake in uncovering the large truths—to discover what had really happened to his sister— only heightened the dramtic tension, and continues to serve as a subtext for the whole series.

He's someone who urgently wants to believe that there are aliens and things beyond our earthly understanding, partly because the alternative—that the government and its bureaucracy can be so full of evil—is really a more hateful proposition to have to swallow, even when he knows it's true.

So David has chosen to portray Mulder as someone very human. He's not a superhero, able to leap large conspiracies in a single bound. Rather, he's frail, with foibles, wrong ideas. When Mulder is in a fight—and the show is decidedly more cerebral than physical—he's usually the person on the losing end. Those characteristics—the overall uncertainty, meshed with the intelligence, and the willingness to follow hunches, is something that molded itself perfectly around David's low-key acting style. In other roles, he seemed withdrawn and reserved at times, removed from the proceedings. As Mulder, he's shown that a man can be heroic without having to be macho, that things can be solved without force.

His increasing fame brought with it a few other opportunities, like the chance to appear on one of his favorite televison shows, the HBO comedy series, "The Larry Sanders Show," starring Garry Shandling. With filming for "The X-Files" season over, David had the time to do it, so when the offer came, he jumped at it. (It's actually his second favorite—"NYPD

Blue" remains appointment viewing in *his* household.)

The show is a parody of the late-night talk shows, a genre Shandling knew all too well, having been on them often enough, both as a comedian and a fill-in host.

David did have one stipulation, however. If he was to be a guest, he wanted to play himself—but as a jerk, a parody of the whole idea of celebrity.

Shandling agreed, and when the script was complete, David came across as someone on a complete star trip—aggressive, demanding, foul-mouthed, and centered only on himself; not just a jerk, but a complete jerk.

That he could play humor was known from his small roles in *Don't Tell Mom the Babysitter's Dead* and *Beethoven*, as well as the deadpan witticisms that were finding their way more and more into "The X-Files." Whether he could pull it off when he was playing himself was a different manner. His friends knew that David was funny, but it was a very dry humor, not unlike the one-liners Mulder tended to throw out.

It walked a razor's edge. David could either have come across as hilarious in the part—and it was, after all, supposed to be him—or as an actor whose arrogance had taken over his ego. It was only David going way over the top in his acting—such a change from his normal style!—that managed to bring it off as riotously funny.

The show turned out to be a feather in his cap, and also brought him a new friend in Garry Shandling. It turned out that they both loved to play basketball, which they did in the downtime between shots, or after rehearsal.

"He has a good outside shot," Shandling quipped, "is aggressive on the court and plays without pants."

It was an outlet for a different, more playful side of his personality. It never worried him for a moment that viewers might believe that the character on "The Larry Sanders Show" was the *real* David. It was simply a bit of fun, an outlet in a life which had been made "a bit more enclosed, a bit more insular" by encroaching stardom.

Still, he honestly didn't resent the fans. A lot of them impressed him.

"They send me really thoughtful things," he said, "and they seem really intelligent. They send me intelligent symposiums on the show."

But after playing Mulder all week, David needed his time to decompress, to try and find himself again, over the weekend, over the summer—actually the spring—and try to regain some balance. It was the same problem he'd run into at the end of the first season.

This time, though, he was a little stronger, which was just as well, since the demands on him were greater. He was a known face, a very popular, handsome face, and he was learning that that brought some responsibilities. Magazines continued to want interviews, there were photo calls to answer, all of them eating into his precious free time.

"That's hard," he said, ". . . because the job takes a lot of time and energy and interviews take more time, energy. You take your alloted amount of energy and do the best work you can. Sometimes you have to explain how you don't have anything left for the media."

He'd gone back to L.A. for the off-season, to be with Perrey, a relationship which was still good and solid, to enjoy having some time around her again, and to see if this year the place seemed any more homelike to him. It didn't. Work had made him a real nomad. Home had become the last place he hung his jacket.

He was too exhausted, and too busy, to take any movie roles during his break, although scripts "in all genres" were deluging his agent. There was no surer sign that he'd arrived, that he'd become a star, than to be in constant demand. There was a publicity trip to New York to do a few interviews at the Four Seasons Hotel. Then back to the West Coast for some real rest and relaxation with Perrey before it was time to make the journey north again.

The second season of "The X-Files" had pulled the show out of cult status and quite squarely into the mainstream. Even people who didn't watch it knew it existed, and knew where they could find it if they wanted to give it a try. Outside America they were eating it up. At first it had been a handful of countries, with dialogue dubbed into a few languages. Now it was up to sixty countries, with more languages than David really wanted to consider. He wasn't just famous in America. He'd become a global face. Everybody wanted him now.

"But you know," he said, "it is more satisfying to me to deal with the people who tried to help me a long time ago, who believed in me, who told me to just hang in there."

He knew he wanted to go back to work, that he'd come to really love the part he'd initally rejected, that had become him, but that didn't mean he was always thrilled at what was necessary to make it happen, to go back to Vancouver and be alone with Blue again, to have a life submerged in work.

"There are some days," he said, "when it is really a terrible prospect to me."

But in truth, there was plenty to look forward to. "The X-Files" had achieved a sort of critical mass of popularity. The ratings had grown throughout the second season, and then grown even more during the summer reruns, as it continued to be a breakout program. Word of mouth and press about the show and David had fueled the spiral, bringing in more curious people, until it looked as if a real impact on the Nielsen numbers was inevitable.

The Fox network was so pleased with what had happened that they'd contracted for three more seasons, which in turn meant employment—at a substantially higher salary—for David, as well as Gillian.

With the increased popularity, there was also an increased budget, allowing the technical staff to do things they'd never been able to manage before, and to handle the old things in a more subtle manner.

But the bottom line, as Carter emphasized over and over again, was quality. "We want to get back to what we do best, which is telling good, scary stories, and telling them in ways that are completely unfamiliar. . . We're trying to break out of [the] mold. The paranormal is the paranormal. UFOs are UFOs. Those are the staples of the show. Those stories are the lifeblood of the show, but we'll come at them differently. We'll tell stories about ESP, reincarnation, psychokinesis, any of these things that have become the most identifiable part of paranormal, unexplained phenomena. We will use those things, but use them in different ways. You will see themes, but you will also see them treated in new ways. I think this is what *really* distinguishes the show . . ."

Keeping it all going, and going well, was the main problem that Carter had to handle now, as he knew only too well: "The trick will be to keep reinventing the work that we do."

So far they'd succeeded. They'd been constantly refining the concepts and the characters. Mulder himself had softened from the prickly personality he'd been when the show began. He was still distant, but he'd shown himself capable of opening up to Scully. There was a definite warmth slowly emerging from the reserve.

Many had continued to wonder about a potential romance between the two agents. After all, there was no denying that electricity—of whatever sort—buzzed between them when they were on-screen. But from the very beginning, as Carter had insisted, it had been a non-issue. Mulder and Scully were professional colleagues. There'd be trust and friendship, but that would be as far as it could ever go. For television it made a refreshing change, and certainly David was happy with the idea.

"The characters' bond is just as good as sleeping together," he explained to *Entertainment Weekly*. "If we progress into a [sexual] relationship, that becomes the focus of the show. And then it becomes like any other show which focuses on a boring relationship between two white people."

Gillian's view on it was equally firm.

"If [a romance] ever happens, it would be the last show," she said. "Writers are adamant about keeping it platonic."

For Carter, the male-female pairing had never meant romance.

"I'm interested in male and female relationships generally," he said. "I think they're the most interesting relationships in life. They're non-competitive and can be, beyond anything romantic, more interesting and honest. It's a very natural relationship, and one where people can do their best for reasons that go beyond sex or romance, but for the complementary elements of the relationship."

Off the set, the relationship David and Gillian enjoyed greatly resembled the one they acted. They were perfectly friendly. "But," he said, "we don't hang out. We are very wary of the fact that at any moment the other can turn into a psychotic human being because of the demands that are put on us, the sixteen-hour days. So I know when she is tired and irritable, and she knows the same about me. We have a great respect for the fine line the other is walking all the time."

And Gillian pointed out that they did have their ups and downs with each other.

"We both tend to be quite moody, but underneath I think we care about each other."

That really came through in the rapport they enjoyed before the cameras.

"The way Mulder and Scully are on-screen is the way David and Gillian are in person," wardrobe supervisor Gillian Kieft observed. "They help each other, they respect each other."

That was how it had developed, and how it would continue. Professional, respectful, and thoughtful.

They'd both succeeded in ways they could never have imagined when they first read the script for the pilot.

"I didn't think it would go," David said. "I lost. But, you know, I won, too."

Indeed, the whole show had become a massive winner, something which had tapped into the zeitgeist all over the globe. And now it was time to go and do it again, and make it better than ever.

TEN

Merge:
Fame

When the third season of "The X-Files" began, on September 22, 1995, it more than picked up where it left off. "The Blessing Way" continued from the cliffhanger of David's "Anasazi," but with the kind of confidence that only a show at the top of its strength could manage.

And why not? It had gone well beyond being a hit in America, or even just in places where English was the first language. By now, viewers crowded around their television sets every week in more than sixty countries to watch the latest episode, often bizarrely dubbed into the local language.

In Finland it was "Salaiset Kansiot" ("The Secret Files"), in Taiwan "X-Dang An." The French preferred to call it "Aux Frontières du

Réel," "At the Borders of Reality," while the Germans deemed it "Ake X—Die Unheimlichen Faelle des FBI"—"The Uncanny Files of the FBI."

Whatever name you gave it, though, one thing was certain—"The X-Files" had arrived in a massive way. The summer had seen the first "X-Files" conventions in the U.S., bringing out thousands of the faithful, who were willing to pay up to $20 to be able to buy merchandise, listen to Chris Carter and others speak about the show, and fraternize with other X-Philes.

It wasn't entirely without precedent—"Star Trek" conventions had been packing them in for years—but no show had managed to have such an impact after only two years.

And by its very nature, the popularity the show enjoyed extended to its stars, David in particular. He was a bona fide celebrity, a hunk, the object of more fantasies than probably even he would care to imagine.

He was also very much in demand. His schedule in Vancouver was no less gruelling than it had been when he first started on the show, but now there were all the other requests, for appearances on "Late Night with David Letterman," "Saturday Night Live," and so many others. Certainly many, many more than he could humanly manage.

But "The X-Files" came first; there was never

any doubt in his mind about that. Anything else he did would have to fit around it. That was the bottom line.

The show was just getting better and better. The writers were taking more chances. They had the viewers who would stay with them now, so they could become wilder than ever, create even greater conspiracies than before: a Japanese scientist who experimented on aliens with government approval, and who'd been Scully's abductor; an insurance salesman in Minneapolis with ESP.

They'd also allowed Mulder to loosen up a little. There were more wisecracks and one-liners, albeit still in that deadpan voice of David's. He was even seen to smile a little on camera, and once or twice let a wide grin slide across his face. Mulder's look had been softened, too. For the first couple of seasons his hair had been in a sharp cut, all angles and edges, very businesslike. Now it was allowed to fall a little more, to seem more natural. Everything was more relaxed.

And Mulder's character was allowed to open up a little, too. There was the obvious attraction he felt for Bambi, the entomologist who specialized in cockroaches. Of course, it couldn't come to anything, as she left with another scientist (and Mulder had to take a lot of ribbing from Scully about wanting someone called Bambi in the first place), but it was still an indication of the way the show was evolving.

Without a doubt, there was the freedom to change their approach now. David and Gillian had both signed contracts to stay with the show until the end of the 1997–98 season, indicating that the show was on very secure footing. They could afford to throw caution to the winds, even let David's natural sense of humor percolate through to a small extent.

"The X-Files" had become big business, bigger than just television; Hollywood even wanted a part of it. If it was successful on TV, the thinking went, just imagine how it could pack 'em in at the multiplexes. And so a deal was signed for an "X-Files" movie—the only drawback being that it couldn't be shot until 1997, given that both David and Gillian already had commitments for the upcoming off-season. That made the movie a gamble: Could "The X-Files" continue, or possibly even grow, in popularity for that long? If it did, then it would pay off handsomely. If not, then the studio would be chalking up another loss.

For the moment, though, it all looked safe. "The X-Files" was growing into a behemoth. Merchandise sales were booming. Comics based on the series were becoming collectors' items almost as soon as they appeared. People all over the globe were searching for "X-Files" sites on the World Wide Web, and more sites dedicated to the show were appearing every week.

But what really mattered was that not only did the show sustain the level of quality it had established, it got better.

Chris Carter had said, "I never want anything to be familiar on this show," and nothing was. It remained a voyage into the unknown every Friday night, and more and more people were coming along for the ride.

The partnership of Mulder and Scully remained exactly that. David was getting more attention in the press, he was the resident hunk who received fan mail from all over the globe, but the two agents were very much a team. No one on the show wanted it to be the Fox Mulder hour with Dana Scully. The chemistry that propelled "The X-Files" came from the two of them together, his intuition and her logic, the little verbal spars, and the trust that had built up between them. To have altered that would have spelled disaster, in exactly the same manner that a romance between them would.

And so the show settled in for its third season roller-coaster ride of thrills, more than a few chills, and the pursuit of the truth that was out there.

As *Entertainment Weekly* said in December, 1995, "Well into its third season, 'X-Files' shows no sign of flagging inspiration; its ability to find paranoia in the paranormal appears to be limitless."

The magazine also noted the "gratifying fine-tuning" which had been given to Mulder and Scully, noting that Fox "isn't nearly as much of a dour lump as he used to be."

Nor was it just the populist publications which were taking an interest in the show. Suddenly the intellectuals were sniffing around, too, finally admitting that "The X-Files" had some weight, something for the mind to snack on as well as the eye. *America* was happy to recommend "a show that might have flown under your radar, as it were."

The reviewer was right in pointing out the fact that it tended to appeal to a younger audience with its emphasis on "the different, the bizarre," and also the "popular suspicions of an overarching Government conspiracy—as favored by older adolescents like Oliver Stone."

"But," he continued, "it's clearly the characters of Mulder and Scully who cement the show: they're brainy, dedicated and articulate. And, for once, the big question about this working couple isn't 'Will they sleep together?' Instead, it's 'Will they catch the bad guys?' Or, in this case, bad things."

Commonweal, too, had turned its steely gaze towards the television on a Friday night, finding "The X-Files" to be "one of the very closest approaches TV has made to the shiver of confronting faerie . . . But the stunning goodness of the show was in the original concept of executive producer Chris Carter."

As for Mulder, the magazine saw in him "a parable about Religious Man in the Age of Perfect Information. For all the transformation of the world into pure data, Mulder still feels the terror and allure of the world as Mystery, a visionary trapped in the infonet."

That might have been reading a lot into it, but it did contain more than a grain of truth, and it was more colorful than *America*'s observation that "Mr. Duchovny plays Fox as an intelligent, taciturn, methodical man."

The truth was that David still played Mulder as a man with an underlying mission—to discover what had happened to his sister. All the rest was either incidental, or information gathered along the way. Fox was on a journey, a Knight of the Round Table, if you like, seeking his personal grail.

David's own quest was a little more mundane: to be known as an actor, to find the balance in roles between substance and commerce. The popularity of "The X-Files" was giving him that. He'd become a known face. His name had some power to it now. He could do pretty much what he wanted, and he could show the other facets of his character, such as his appearance on Garry Shandling's comedy show—or on "Saturday Night Live."

In its early days, "Saturday Night Live" had been groundbreaking comedy. But the shine had long since tarnished, and the show had limped along for several years, throwing up occasional stars, and others who thought they might be stars.

Maybe David had fond memories of "SNL"'s glory days. Or perhaps he wanted to flex his comedic muscles a little more. Whatever the reason, he accepted the offer to host the show.

The writing played to his strengths, letting him be his low-key self, performing a sketch about a Richard Gere-like actor which required little more than using exaggerated facial expressions. His opening monologue brought huge applause, and it *was* funny, including some videotape. For the most part, though, he was just there, like all the cast members, wading through a fairly endless sea of mediocrity and introducing the musical guest—Rod Stewart—which might not have been a huge thrill to a man who was constantly buying CDs and listening to *new* music.

Other than brief forays like those, though, his focus had to remain squarely on the show. David was a real professional. He knew all too well that the only reason Letterman and "SNL" were interested in him was because "The X-Files" had made him into a star. If he blew that, he blew everything.

And he wasn't about to do that. The success

had astonished him, but that didn't mean it wasn't welcome.

The long days of filming in Vancouver were no less gruelling than they had been before, but now the point was much more obvious. During its second season, "The X-Files" had increased its audience by 44 per cent. It had established itself in the pantheon of modern popular culture, and David was very much a part of that.

He didn't feel any more at home in Vancouver these days than he had before, but there was now at least a familiarity about it.

"I think the last place I leave I look on as home," he told *Details*, "even though while I'm there it doesn't feel that way. It's what Proust said about Milton: 'The only true paradise is paradise lost.'"

But in a way, David had just entered paradise—at least what would be paradise for some. Feted, desired, talked and written about, he was on the receiving end of American celebrity in the late twentieth century, where celebrity was almost akin to worship. To a viewing audience that increased every Friday, he *was* Fox Mulder.

By acting, being in movies and on television, he'd courted fame. Now she was bestowing her favors, and David was discovering it wasn't quite everything he'd hoped. But he'd come to realize, "I don't think I have a choice at this point." He was caught up in the beast.

It didn't leave him the room to be human, to be silly, or make mistakes. When he was out, he was constantly under the microscope. And he found that uncomfortable. All his privacy was gone.

At the same time he was grateful. The show gave him the economic security he'd never enjoyed before, and he was involved with something that was well-done, adventurous, that had depth and ideas—perfect fodder for a former graduate student whose mind was still very active.

He understood and had analyzed some of its appeal, just how much the show tapped into the zeitgeist.

"I think 'The X-Files' is very nineties," he said, "because everything is left in doubt. There's no closure, no answers."

Which was perfectly true. A case might be solved, but there was always a bigger question behind it—how could this have happened in the first place? Mulder and Scully might win some battles, but the war, it seemed, would always continue.

And while "The X-Files" was a series of its time, so was David's life. He'd become nomadic, a sublet here, a sublet there, very few possessions or attachments holding him down, no real sense of connection, no real roots anymore. Beyond his family, Perrey, and his dog, Blue, there wasn't even the weight of relationships. And none of those kept him tied to the spot. But roots and history didn't really matter much any more, in life, even in music.

"I don't have a taste for straight-up stuff like that," he explained. "I prefer the Stones to the people they were covering. There are people who listen to the Red Hot Chili Peppers because they never heard Jimi Hendrix or George Clinton. There is no history now. Nobody cares to go back even two years. When I was growing up, the focus was on who were the originals and who were the visionaries. Originality is not something to agonize over any more."

And perhaps he was right; originality as a quality wasn't that necessary for the nineties. But mixing the elements that had gone before in a new way, then adding something of your own, *was*. "The X-Files" had done that quite successfully, taking bits of "The Outer Limits," "Kolchak: The Night Stalker," even "Star Trek," and stirring them all together before adding its own ingredients to create something faintly familiar but still quite exotic and unique.

What David has brought to the show has been an important factor in creating this new hybrid. His style, mixing the serious with the deadpan, has injected a very human element into the series. The chemistry in Mulder's relationship with Scully helps bring viewers back. Every episode is a buddy movie, just as much as "Butch Cassidy and the Sundance Kid" was.

It's just in the way it's all come together, the fit of the pieces, and, as David pointed out, its timing, that's made it so successful.

"The belief in other worlds is a time-honored human endeavor," David told *Playboy*. People want to believe. Many *need* to believe. And, in the guise of Mulder, David helps them believe, week after week.

In return, they've made a star out of him. Mulder and David have become inextricably linked now. To viewers, where one stops and the other begins is a very grey, fuzzy line, if they even care.

"I would like to see Fox Mulder take on a life of his own," David mused about the future, "and actually have a Joseph Campbell journey, rather than have him merely play through a series of unrelated experiences. I see it more as an interior journey. . . . How do we heal him? How do we show him the truth?"

Could it happen? Probably not. Television has its requirements, and however much "The X-Files" might push the envelope, it's not going to burst it entirely. The psychological drama of Mulder's voyage of discovery might make a good book, a fine romantic quest, but it would never play on a screen, small or large.

Fox Mulder will remain pretty much as written. He'll develop, of course, and perhaps he'll eventually come closer to learning what really happened to Samantha; maybe as its final episode, "The X-Files" will give him the release of understanding. But in the end, the truth will still remain out there.

Fox Mulder has become David's signature role. For better or worse, it's the way people have come to see him. All the movies that went before have become history, little more than a run-up to the main event. But sometime, be it when his new contract expires, or at some other point down the line, "The X-Files" will end. No series can last forever. And then his challenge will be just beginning.

But the show has established him. "E! Entertainment" found him to be one of the "World's Sexiest Men" (originally he made the grade in the "Take Him Home to Mother" category; after some consideration they upgraded him to "Classy"). He's won awards for his portrayal of Mulder.

To a point he'll probably never be able to outrun Mulder. The shadow has become larger than life. But that can be a help, too, as much as a hindrance. He's in demand. He's *hot.* The starring movie roles are being offered.

When the time comes for Mulder to hang up his gun, it won't be the end for David Duchovny. He'll simply have moved onward and upward. There'll be movies with his name above the title. He'll have reached that new level he couldn't climb to before the series. Life will go on, very likely better than before. He'll be able to take the parts he really wants, rather than whatever comes along to pay the bills.

He'll be able to mix commerce and art as much as he pleases. And it'll all be because he took a role in a television pilot that he didn't think would interfere with his movie career.

Conclusion
Close File. Exit

"The X-Files" had done what the movies failed to do: make David Duchovny into a household name. It's given him the opportunity to do pretty much whatever he wants—and there's still plenty he wants to do.

He's signed for his first starring role in a film, to portray a Mafia doctor in "Playing God," which will be shot as soon as the third season of the show is over.

"There's enough time," he said, "but everything has to work out perfectly."

All too often when the big names of television try to make that transition to film star, things don't work out. What projects in one medium doesn't necessarily play well in another. But David is very much a special case. Films are his background; they were his ladder up, his apprenticeship. It's not a problem that should plague him.

And he's been careful, waiting for the right part, not grabbing the first script that came along. He has that luxury now, and he intends to make it work for him.

And the filming will serve more than one purpose in his life. Apart from putting $2 million in his pocket, it'll keep him from spending his two-month vacation feeling like a stateless man in Los Angeles again. True, it means he'll be more nomadic than ever, as well as less rested, but he'll have work to occupy his mind. Which may also help his personal life, since the rumors of a split between David and Perrey have grown rife, and he's started the time-honored ritual of escorting gorgeous actresses around—in this case Kristin Davis, who plays Brooke on "Melrose Place."

But it'll be a long while before the time to brood catches up with him. After the fourth season of "The X-Files," he and Gillian are both signed to star in an "X-Files" movie, which means that his calendar remains fully booked until 1998—an enviable position for any actor, but especially for one who dropped into it late and without any real purpose. It might have taken him a few years, but David has definitely arrived in style.

*   *   *

As a celebrity he can even indulge his passion for basketball on camera. In 1994 he took part in MTV's "Rock 'n' Jock Basketball" game (although neither a rocker nor a jock), showing, as he had on "Red Shoe Diaries," more than a touch of skill at slamming hoops.

But perhaps the biggest surprise, the strangest turn, was David becoming a model. Mulder had no reputation for walking the cutting edge of fashion on television, preferring government basic blue or grey, albeit in a flattering cut, and even David's most ardent fans had wondered about his choice of suit for the 1995 Golden Globe Awards. So when Saks Fifth Avenue asked him to display the expensive designer labels in their "Men's Designer" fall catalog for 1995, as part of a new campaign using celebrities to sell clothes, it was a shock.

Still he did it, quite gamely, even with a smile on his face as he was photgraphed in fluted collars and suits that would never pass the FBI dress code, adding yet another string to his bow.

He's broken through, not merely to that next level, but to the upper echelons. His face, his name, his show, have all become familiar worldwide. And the show is helping to make him a rich man. Not in the Michael Jackson league, but at a reported $100,000 per episode, it's putting him into a bracket where he'll never need to work again. So, when "The X-Files" is over, as it surely will be one day, and David's taken off Mulder's suit for the final time, what then?

"I feel I've got ten more years of playing the guy," he told a reporter. "When I'm forty-five, I'll start thinking about what else I want to do."

Maybe it'll be that long, maybe not; ten years is almost an eternity in show business. In between there'll be plenty of chances for David to do more writing for the show, and quite possibly some directing, too, although whether he'll end up doing those to stave off boredom even he's not certain.

"Being offered story lines and directing, it reminds me of playing with my dog. I'll give him a choice between a tennis ball or a Frisbee—whatever it takes to keep him involved."

But he does firmly believe that writing will play a part in his future, whether it's getting back to what he humorously calls "his roots" as a graduate student and finally finishing off that old PhD dissertation and going on to teach, or possibly returning to playwriting.

"I want to get back to plays someday when I have the time for a sustained effort."

Certainly writing, and possibly directing, would help satisfy some of the constant intellectual appetite that David has.

Almost certainly there'll be more romance. The rumors about his split with Perrey—or, more accurately, her split from him—remain unconfirmed, so perhaps the relationship will continue. But if not, there'll be others. Maybe even marriage and children somewhere in the future. But the image of David meshes with the image of Mulder, or Jake on "Red Shoe Diaries," in the end he's always walking alone, or with his dog. The consummate outsider, as David has always been, right from childhood.

Whatever the future might hold, though, for now, David's on top of the television heap. Along with Gillian, he was picked by *TV Guide* as one of 1995's Best Performers on television, "lighting up TV's scariest drama with humor and sexual desire." It's just one of many accolades coming to David, and to "The X-Files." While it's made a major figure out of David, he's also now been one of the reasons for its success, drawing in female viewers with his looks and his body, and keeping the watchers tuning back in with Mulder's sly, dry sense of humor.

He took the role and made it completely his own in a manner that rarely happens on television. From the very beginning it fit him well, and with just a few adjustments over the first couple of seasons, the fit became perfect.

And from what he's said, there's little chance of David abandoning Mulder before the show has run its course. His initial commitment to the character, and the series, might have been reluctant, but once he'd made it, he was there for the long haul, wanting to make it the best that he can. He's not a prima donna, ready to abandon ship at the first offer of something bigger. "The X-Files" has made him, and he understands that all too well. He's loyal to the show, and will remain that way.

He has no reason not to be. The producers allow him time for the small humorous side projects, indulging his appearances with Garry Shandling or performing a voice-over for the USA Network cartoon "Duckman." Or even commercials—he recently appeared in an ad for NYNEX. But those aren't exactly work for David; more a relief valve from the constant pressure to produce an excellent program week after week. Now the standards have been set on "The X-Files," they have to be kept up, and even raised—if that's possible.

It's a long journey from the Lower East Side to the quiet halls of academia, then on to the cheer of the crowds in Los Angeles, or even in Vancouver. And it's one that very few have made. It takes courage to turn your back, to walk away after working so long towards something you believed you wanted, then to start afresh, at the bottom of the heap, in one of the world's chanciest professions.

But it was what David felt in his heart that he had to do, so he did it. By now he could have been a tenured professor, teaching literature at a university somewhere, on the receiving end of so many co-ed fantasies, writing monographs and books, and establishing a reputation as a literary critic of the first order. Some of his plays might even have been produced. There would have been security in all that, a straight path to follow through life.

Instead, he's been up, and down, and now he's up again, higher than he might ever have expected. In 1993, after *Kalifornia*, he was wondering when and if his shot at the big time would come. Well, it arrived, and after an initial hesitation, he grabbed it and held on.

If the figures are correct, David makes well over $1 million a year from "The X-Files." He'll receive another $2 million for his next movie role. It's not in the Bruce Willis class, but it's certainly not minimum wage, either. And for someone who, just four years ago, was having to take any part offered to pay the rent and establish himself, it's a great jump.

Right now, David has it all. The adulation, the critical praise, the awards, and the opportunities; he's hitting on every level, commercial and artistic. *Very* few people have been able to achieve that. For some it would be easy to get caught up in it all, to believe all the words on paper or flying through cyberspace. David, though, keeps his feet firmly planted on the ground.

"Ultimately you realize that you're being appreciated for something that doesn't have much to do with you. . . . There are two things I don't want to do in my spare time," he said.

"One is talk about 'The X-Files' and the other is think about how people are perceiving me."

He's made it to the top of the hill, where he can look down on the past and the future. He's made the climb through hard work, the grit most actors need to wade through. That he's managed to come so far is an inspiration for others starting in the profession. But talent will out, they say, and that's something David's shown that he has in abundance.

Add to that a strong sense of the absurd, and you have a star who makes no ego demands, who laughs at himself as much as others, and who refuses to take the whole thing seriously. There are no star trips for David.

"So now that I'm finally beginning to understand [the star trip]. . . I wanted to play it. That's why I did the thing with Garry."

The camera loves him, as it does all stars. But that doesn't mean David loves the camera; he'd rather grin at it. And that's undoubtedly how he'll stay. The truth might well be out there, but David is very much here.

When "The X-Files" finishes its run, whether that's when David's contract expires and he decides to explore other options, or ten years from now, he'll move on with a sly grin and a wry word, the nomad, the smiling loner with his dog.

And that's exactly how everyone would want it to be.

Acknowledgments

As always, I'm indebted to the many people who've helped directly and indirectly with the writing of this book. Madeleine Morel, a goddess among agents, for brokering the deal. Ann McKay Thoroman, my editor, for believing and going to bat on the thing. The "X-Philes" who live at America Online, whose gossip and speculation proved a vital source. Dave Thompson might have jeered good naturedly, but his heart was in the right place, his eyes were open, and without him none of my books might ever have happened. Dennis Wilken, Mary Hargrove, Thom Atkinson, who offered constant encouragement. In England, as ever, my mother and father, Ray and Betty Nickson, Lee, Greg, and Mike Murtagh. Much closer to home, Linda, whose love and support keep me buoyant, and Graham, our own adventure into the unknown, as well as Junior, Tasha, Boodle, Zuni, Mardi, and Bina.

A lot of articles proved to be valuable resources. Foremost among them were: "No Wonder He's Called Fox" by Benjamin Svetkey in *Entertainment Weekly*, September 29, 1995; "The X-Files Exposed," by Dana Kennedy, also in *Entertainment Weekly*, March 10, 1995; "David Duchovny—17 Questions" by Malissa Thompson, *Seventeen*, December 1995; "X-ellence" by Tom Gliatto and Craig Tomashoff, *People*, October 9, 1995; "The X-Man," by Scott Cohen, *Details*, October 1995; "X-Factor Actor" by Jack Hitt, *Playboy*, November 1995; "Gillian and Dave's X-cellent Adventure," by Deborah Starr Seibel, *TV Guide*, March 11, 1995; "David Duchovny," by James Grant, *Cosmopolitan*, October 1995; "A Genuine X-entric," by Bruce Fretts, *Entertainment Weekly*, December 2, 1994; "Going to X-tremes," by Michael A. Lipton, *People*, April 25, 1994. And finally, N.E. Genge's *The Unofficial 'X-Files' Companion*, (Crown trade paperback, 1995) and *The Truth Is Out There: The Official Guide to 'The X-Files'* by Brian Lowry (Harper Prism 1995).

Zecharia Sitchin's
The Earth Chronicles

BOOK I: THE 12TH PLANET
39362-X/$6.99 US/$8.99 CAN

This revolutionary work brings together lost, antediluvian texts, ancient cosmologies, and newly discovered celestial maps to reach the shocking conclusion that we are descendants of a superior race from the 12th planet.

BOOK II: THE STAIRWAY TO HEAVEN
63339-6/$6.99 US/$8.99 CAN

BOOK III: THE WARS OF GODS AND MEN
89585-4/$6.99 US/$8.99 CAN

BOOK IV: THE LOST REALMS
75890-3/$6.99 US/$8.99 CAN

BOOK V: WHEN TIME BEGAN
77071-7/$6.99 US/$8.99 CAN

And Don't Miss the Companion Volumes:

GENESIS REVISITED: IS MODERN SCIENCE CATCHING UP WITH ANCIENT KNOWLEDGE?
76159-9/$6.99 US/$8.99 CAN

DIVINE ENCOUNTERS: A GUIDE TO VISIONS, ANGELS, AND OTHER EMISSARIES
78076-3/$6.50 US/$8.50 CAN

Astonishing UFO Reports
from Avon Books

COMMUNION: A TRUE STORY
by Whitley Strieber 70388-2/$6.99 US/$8.99 Can

TRANSFORMATION: THE BREAKTHROUGH
by Whitley Strieber 70535-4/$4.95 US/$5.95 Can

THE GULF BREEZE SIGHTINGS
by Ed Walters and Frances Walters
70870-1/$6.99 US/$8.99 Can

UFO ABDUCTIONS IN GULF BREEZE
by Ed Walters and Frances Walters
77333-3/$4.99 US/$5.99 Can

THE UFO CRASH AT ROSWELL
by Kevin D. Randle and Donald R. Schmitt
76196-3/$5.99 US/$7.99 Can

THE TRUTH ABOUT THE UFO CRASH AT ROSWELL
by Kevin D. Randle and Donald R. Schmitt
77803-3/$6.99 US/$8.99 Can

A HISTORY OF UFO CRASHES
by Kevin D. Randle 77666-9/$5.99 US/$7.99 Can

Sex Education
for young people aged 11–18
a quick guide
for parents and carers

Janice Slough

Series Advisers

Gerald Haigh   Writer and Consultant in Education

Pauline Maskell   Secondary Head of Health Studies

John Sutton   General Secretary, Secondary Heads Association

Advisory Panel

Ruth Joyce   Adviser on Drugs and Health Education

Mike Kirby   Writer on Education

Terry Saunders   Secondary Head of Biology

Anne Morgan   Primary Deputy Headteacher

Elaine Wilson   Secondary Head of Science

ISBN: 1 85467 313 0

© 1995

Daniels Publishing
38 Cambridge Place
Cambridge CB2 1NS

I like the idea of Quick Guides. Teachers need reliable information and advice on a very wide range of subjects related to their work and they need it to be accessible and concise. This series attempts to meet those needs by drawing on the knowledge of experienced practitioners and presenting the essential material in a format which facilitates rapid reference and provides valuable action checklists.

I am sure that these guides will be useful to teachers, to governors, to parents and indeed to all who are concerned with the effective management of all aspects of education.

John Sutton
General Secretary
Secondary Heads Association

Sex Education, ages 11–18: a quick guide

Janice Slough is a consultant and trainer in Personal and
Social Education. She is based on the Isle of Wight, and
has previously worked as a teacher, youth worker and
health education co-ordinator.

Contents

Sex Education, ages 11–18: a quick guide

Introduction

Secondary school students are at a crucial stage in their lives: they are changing from children into adults. Sexual maturing is central to this change and so it is important that young people understand what is happening to their bodies and the emotional and social changes they will go through.

Parents are often concerned about how best to help their children through adolescence. Given that young people are subject to such varied influences and messages about sex, home and school must work together to protect them against ignorance, distress, and even exploitation.

This Quick Guide interprets the significance of the Education Act 1993: Sex Education in Schools for parents, carers and young people. Much of the material in the Quick Guide draws on the Department for Education's *Circular 5/94: The Education Act 1993: Sex Education in Schools* and the National Curriculum Council document *Curriculum Guidance 5: Health Education.* There is also some material from the NCC's *Curriculum Guidance 8: Education for Citizenship.*

The 1993 Act, which sets out the framework for school sex education, emphasises the importance of parents in the sex education and sexual health of their children. It states that sex education in schools should complement and support the role of parents and others who have legal responsibility for the young person.

The Act, together with the circular and the curriculum guidance documents, applies to all state primary, middle, secondary and special schools, including grant-maintained and voluntary-aided schools. It does not cover private schools unless they choose to follow the directives voluntarily.

Circular 5/94 says 'Parents are key figures in helping their children to cope with the emotional and physical aspects of growing up and preparing them for the challenges and responsibilities which sexual maturity brings.'

This Quick Guide deals with concerns parents may have about sex education and suggests ways in which parents and carers can help their teenagers through the difficult adolescent years to meet the challenges and responsibilities of growing up into sexual maturity.

This Quick Guide contains:

- [ ] a summary of the relevant legislation for Key Stages 3 and 4 (11–18 years).

- [ ] the rationale and principles of sex education.

- [ ] the possible content and organisation of sex education in schools at Key Stages 3 and 4.

- [ ] ideas for how parents might respond to the Act.

- [ ] practical advice on how parents can help their teenagers.

Throughout this Quick Guide, the term 'parent' refers to all those who are guardians or carers of young people.

✓ You may find it useful to tick the boxes when each task is completed.

We would welcome constructive comments on this booklet. Please address them to the publisher.

☐ 'Sex education is about relating to other people, respecting the rights and feelings of others, and developing loving caring relationships as friends, parents, members of a family and sexual partners. It also involves learning to say "no" to unwanted sexual advances and to protect oneself from abuse and exploitation.' The Family Planning Association

☐ 'To provide knowledge about loving relationships, the nature of sexuality and the processes of human reproduction.' *Circular 5/94*

☐ 'It should lead to the acquisition of understanding and attitudes which prepare pupils to view their relationships in a responsible and healthy manner. It must not be value free.' *Circular 5/94*

☐ 'To prepare pupils to cope with the physical and emotional challenges of growing up.' *Circular 5/94*

☐ 'It provides knowledge about the processes of reproduction and the nature of sexuality and relationships. It encourages the acquisition of skills and attitudes which allow pupils to manage their relationships in a responsible and healthy manner.' *Curriculum Guidance 5*

Why sex education is important

'Young people have the right to know about how their bodies work, and to learn about relating to other people and about protecting themselves from unwanted sexual advances, unwanted pregnancy and STDs.' *The Family Planning Association*

'Sex Education provides an understanding that positive, caring environments are essential for the development of a good self-image and that individuals are in charge of and responsible for their own bodies.' *Curriculum Guidance 5*

'The *Health of the Nation* White Paper identified sexual health as one of the five key areas in which substantial improvement in health could be achieved. Sex education can make a substantial contribution.' *Circular 5/94*

Young people withdrawn from sex education may be most at risk from ignorance, exploitation or sexual abuse.

Parents generally want schools to help with the sex education of their adolescents, especially if they believe young people find talking about sex with parents embarrassing.

Research shows that sex education delays the beginning of young people's sexual activity and increases safer sexual behaviour.

Education about HIV/AIDS dispels myths and prejudices and can be life-saving.

'The importance of sexual relationships in all our lives is such that sex education is a crucial part of preparing children for their lives now and in the future as adults and parents.' Her Majesty's Inspectors' *Curriculum Matters 6*

'It encourages the acquisition of skills and attitudes which allow pupils to manage their relationships in a responsible and healthy manner.' Curriculum Guidance 5.

Good practice in sex education

Sex education at its best is a partnership between home and school.

When planning a sex education programme, schools should consider:
- the age, needs and maturity of the pupils
- cultural and religious factors
- teachers' expertise
- parents' wishes
- school policy
- other professional expertise
- the community served by the school

It is every pupil's entitlement to learn about their developing selves in relationship to others, 'to cope with the physical and emotional challenges of growing up.' *Circular 5/94*

Sex education should be an integral part of health education. There are links between this area, other parts of the curriculum and the whole school ethos.

The foundation of sex education is the development of self-esteem and positive relationships with others.

Sex education should be properly planned and should progress with the student, with areas of work being revisited in different ways to reinforce previous learning.

The law on secondary school sex education

The Education Act 1993, Section 241, states that in mainstream secondary schools:

- Sex education must be provided for all registered pupils, including those over compulsory school age.

- The sex education programme must include education about HIV and AIDS and other sexually transmitted diseases.

- The parents or those who have responsibility for any pupil may if they wish withdraw that pupil from all or part of the sex education provided (unless it is part of compulsory National Curriculum work).

- Schools must have a sex education policy.

- The governing body must keep an up to date written statement of the policy.

- The governing body must inform parents of their right to withdraw children in their care from sex education, and must make the school's sex education policy available to all parents.

- Any sex education must be provided in such a way as to encourage young people to pay attention to moral issues and the value of family life.

'The Government believes that all pupils should be offered the responsibility of receiving a comprehensive, well planned programme of sex education during their school careers...' Circular 5/94.

'Sex education must be provided in such a way as to encourage young people to have regard to moral considerations and the value of family life.' Circular 5/94.

According to the Education Act 1993: Sex Education in Schools, pupils should:

☐ Be encouraged to appreciate
  • the value of stable family life
  • marriage
  • the responsibilities of parenthood
  • the law on sexual behaviour

☐ Be helped to consider the importance of
  • self-restraint
  • respect for themselves and others
  • sensitivity towards the needs and views of others
  • loyalty
  • fidelity

☐ Be enabled to recognise
  • the physical, emotional and moral implications of certain types of behaviour
  • the physical, emotional and moral risks of certain types of behaviour
  • that both sexes must behave responsibly in sexual matters

Sensitive issues in secondary school sex education

Circular 5/94, *Sex Education in Schools*, states that:

☐ Teachers will need to balance the need to cover relevant issues fully with the need to respect pupils' and parents' views and sensitivities.

☐ Care should be taken to match sex education to
- the maturity of the pupils involved
- their capacity to absorb sensitive information
- how important it is for them to have the information at that time.

☐ Young people with learning difficulties may need more help than others to
- cope with the physical and emotional aspects of growing up.
- learn what sorts of behaviour are acceptable
- protect themselves against unacceptable behaviour by adults.

☐ Pupils' questions should be answered sensitively and, if necessary, dealt with outside the classroom, with the parents' consent.

☐ Schools and teachers should be sensitive to religious and cultural factors.

☐ It is not likely to be appropriate for teachers or other professionals to deal with explicit issues raised by an individual pupil with the whole class present.

☐ Teachers, if approached by individual pupils for specific advice, should encourage them to speak to their parents and, if appropriate, a relevant health professional.

☐ Particular care must be taken in relation to contraceptive advice to female pupils under 16, for whom sexual intercourse is illegal.

☐ If a teacher is aware that a pupil's sexual behaviour is likely to place them at moral or physical risk, or break the law, they must make sure the pupil knows the implications and encourage them to get advice. The head teacher should also be informed.

> *'Handling of these matters will place demands on teachers' professional skills.'* Circular 5/94.

'The more successful schools are in achieving... a complementary and supportive role to parents... the less likelihood that parents will wish to exercise their right of withdrawal.' Circular 5/94.

Circular 5/94, *Sex Education in Schools*, states that:

- Parents are key figures in helping their children cope with the physical and emotional changes of growing up and in preparing them for the challenges and responsibilities which sexual maturity brings.
- The sex education offered by schools should complement and support the work of parents.
- The school's sex education policy should be freely available to parents.
- Schools should make sure that parents understand their right to withdraw their child from sex education.
- Schools should show parents their teaching materials and explain the methods that are used in the classroom.
- Parents should be consulted about how explicit the material used should be, and how it should be presented.
- Information about sex education must be included in the school's prospectus.
- The LEA is required to deal with complaints from parents concerning mainstream schools' teaching of sex education.
- Parents of children with special educational needs may find it difficult to come to terms with the idea that their children will become sexually active (although these children need the protection of sex education more than others).
- Schools should take account of the religious and cultural views of students and parents regarding sexuality.
- The teacher's pastoral interest in the welfare of pupils should never trespass on parents' rights and responsibilities.

Parents' right to withdraw their children from school sex education

Circular 5/94, *Sex Education in Schools,* states that:

- A student may be withdrawn by either parent or by any person who has responsibility for or care of the student.

- The right includes all pupils at state schools, including those over compulsory school age.

- Any unresolved dispute between a student and their parent over sex education would have to be referred to the courts.

- Parents do not have to give reasons for their decision or explain what other arrangements they may have in mind.

- Schools should avoid putting any pressure on parents but can invite them to state their reason for withdrawal, so that any misunderstandings can be resolved.

- Once a parent has asked for their child to be withdrawn and the school has complied with their request, the request cannot be changed except by the person who made it.

- Schools should ensure that, if pupils are withdrawn, the rest of their education is not disrupted.

- Parents cannot withdraw their children from those parts of sex education which are part of the National Curriculum Science Order.

'Section 241 of the Education Act 1993 gives parents the right to withdraw their children from any or all parts of a school's programme of sex education, other than those elements which are required by the National Curriculum Science Order.'
Circular 5/94.

The compulsory National Curriculum content of sex education

'**The Secretary of State intends that there should continue to be a requirement for pupils at Key Stage 3 to be taught about human reproduction and the physical and emotional changes that take place during adolescence.'** Circular 5/94.

Parents are not entitled to withdraw their children from this teaching, which forms part of the National Curriculum Order for Science.

Key Stage 3 (11–14 years)

Students should:

- understand the process of reproduction in animals
- study the human life cycle, including the physical and emotional factors humans need in the early stages of development
- begin to make decisions and judgements based on knowledge of issues concerning personal health, well-being and safety.

Key Stage 4 (14–16 years)

Students should:

- extend their knowledge of reproductive organs and processes
- be able to describe how the internal environment is maintained for human embryos
- understand the principles of selective breeding and cloning, and how these give rise to social and ethical issues.

An amendment of 1994 to the programmes of study in the National Curriculum Science Order excludes:

- Acquired Immune Deficiency Syndrome (AIDS) and Human Immunodeficiency Virus (HIV)
- any other sexually transmitted disease
- human sexual behaviour, except biological aspects.

National Curriculum Guidance for Health Education: sex education

National Curriculum Guidance 5: Health Education gives the following advice on what young people should learn about sex education during their secondary school careers.

Key Stage 3 (11–14 years)

☐ Recognise the importance of personal choice in managing relationships so that they do not present risks, for instance to health or to personal safety.

☐ Understand that organisms (including HIV) can be transmitted in many ways, including through sexual activity.

☐ Discuss moral values and explore those held by different cultures and groups.

☐ Understand the concept of stereotyping and identify its various forms.

☐ Be aware of the range of sexual attitudes and behaviour in present-day society.

☐ Understand that people have the right not to be sexually active, and recognise that parenthood is a matter of choice

☐ Know in broad outline the biological and social factors which influence sexual behaviour, and their consequences.

The government advises that young people should learn about the social aspects of sexual behaviour while they are at secondary school.

Key Stage 4 (14–16 years)

- Understand aspects of British law relating to sexual behaviour.

- Understand the biological aspects of reproduction.

- Consider the advantages and disadvantages of various methods of family planning in terms of personal preference and social implications.

- Recognise and be able to discuss sensitive and controversial issues, such as conception, birth, HIV/AIDS, child-rearing, abortion and technological developments, which involve thinking about attitudes, values, beliefs and morality.

- Be aware of the need for preventive health care and know what this involves.

- Be aware of the availability of statutory and voluntary organisations which offer support in human relationships, such as Relate.

- Be aware that feeling positive about sexuality and sexual activity is important in relationships; understand the changes in sexuality during a lifetime and their impact on people's lives, for example the menopause.

- Be aware of partnerships, marriage and divorce, and the impact of loss, separation and bereavement.

- Be able to discuss issues such as sexual harassment in terms of their effects on individuals.

National Curriculum Guidance for Health Education: family life

National Curriculum Guidance 5: Health Education advises that students should learn the following things about family life.

Key Stage 3 (11–14 years)

- Know in more detail [than at Key Stage 2] about child development and the role of primary health care.

- Know about vaccination and immunisation in general health care, for instance protection against disease for children, young people and those travelling abroad.

- Recognise the factors involved in setting up and maintaining a home and planning and having a family; know about the roles of parents and their relationships before and after the arrival of children.

- Recognise the changing nature of relationships within the family due to, for instance, children gaining independence, new members of the family group, and death.

Learning about family life helps to put knowledge about sex into context.

'The principal objective of family life education is that pupils understand and value the central role of the family.' Curriculum Guidance 5.

Key Stage 4 (14–16 years)

☐ Understand the importance of feeling positive about oneself and others.

☐ Be able to express feelings confidently.

☐ Be aware of the part that family life can play in happy and fulfilling relationships.

☐ Be aware of problems which can occur in family life, such as domestic violence, abuse, bereavement, misuse of drugs or other substances, unemployment, illness; be aware of the effects of such problems.

☐ Recognise that some individuals have special needs.

☐ Know about the technology available to influence fertility and be able to discuss the ethical, moral and legal issues involved.

☐ Know in detail, and be able to put into practice, child care skills.

☐ Understand that the roles of different members of the family may alter over time.

☐ Know how to use the helping agencies, such as clinics, hospitals and dentists.

National Curriculum Guidance for Citizenship: family life education

National Curriculum Guidance 8: Education for Citizenship

Pupils' experience of family life is varied. This part of the suggested Citizenship curriculum encourages pupils to understand the nature of family life in all its forms and to distinguish myths and stereotypes from reality. It helps them to examine their current roles, to understand what will be involved if they become partners and parents, and to become more effective in their relationships.

Areas of study might include:

- The importance of the family for physical and spiritual well-being, parenthood and child development, and the fulfilment of emotional and physical needs.

- Family life cycles, patterns of marriage and family structure and how these change.

- Challenges facing family units, such as separation, divorce, domestic problems, or the difficulties of single-parent families.

- Relationships and responsibilities, for instance roles in the home, and the legal and moral responsibilities of parents and children.

- Images of the family and marriage in the media.

'Governors may also find it helpful to take account of the references to family life education in **Curriculum Guidance 8: Education for Citizenship.'** *Circular 5/94.*

Knowledge:

Young people need information which will enable them to understand the processes taking place in their own and other people's bodies and make informed choices.

Skills:

They need to be able to manage their lives for their own and other people's benefit and create healthy relationships.

Attitudes and Values:

They need to understand and empathise with other people and be able to make decisions that are not influenced by prejudice.

'The acquisition of understanding and attitudes which prepare pupils to view their relationships in a responsible and healthy manner.'
Circular 5/94.

Possible content of a secondary sex education programme

Knowledge:

- Puberty; physical and emotional changes
- Personal hygiene
- HIV/AIDS
- Sexually transmitted diseases
- Sex and the law
- Contraception
- Helping agencies
- Keeping safe
- Sexuality
- Parenthood
- Child care and development
- Rights, risks and responsibilities
- Family structures
- Appropriate vocabulary

Skills:

- Coping with: loss, pressures and influences, stress, emotions and feelings
- Building positive relationships
- Assertiveness
- Listening
- Responsibility for oneself
- Dealing with peer pressure
- Negotiation
- Making choices
- Problem solving
- Feeling good about oneself
- Relaxation

A sex education programme must suit the age, needs and maturity of the pupils.

'During
adolescence
especially, skills
concerned with
resisting social
pressures and
respecting the
needs of others
can prove to be as
important as
facts.'
Curriculum
Guidance 5.

Attitudes and Values:

- Positive attitude to one's own sexuality
- Friendship, love and marriage
- Appropriate and inappropriate behaviour
- Stereotyping and prejudice
- Valuing differences and similarities
- Respecting oneself and others
- Attitudes to sensitive and controversial issues, such as abortion, bereavement, disability, gender, abuse, sexual harassment, divorce, ethical and moral issues

It is particularly important that students receive accurate information about HIV and AIDS, and the opportunity to discuss the relevant issues openly, in view of the amount, and unreliability, of media coverage about this subject.

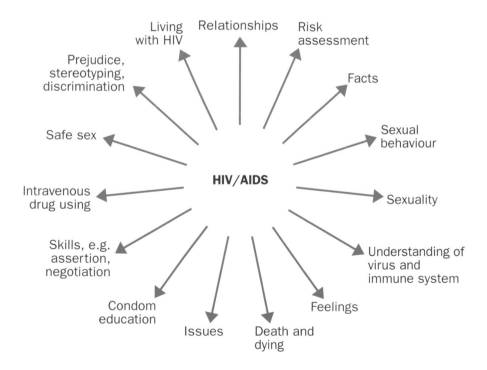

'... helping children to cope with the physical and emotional aspects of growing up.'
Circular 5/94.

Puberty can begin as early as nine years old and may still be going on at 18. Although the physical changes may seem rapid, the emotional and social changes can go on for the whole of adolescence.

The points to stress are:

☐ It is a slow process, and everybody starts and finishes at different times.

☐ There are many different shapes and sizes of breasts, penises and other parts of the body, which are all normal.

☐ Girls usually start developing earlier than boys and remain in advance of them.

Changes that happen to both boys and girls

☐ Growth spurts, in both height and weight; young people may become more clumsy as their bodies adjust to such sudden changes.

☐ Hormonal changes; these affect moods and emotions in unexpected ways and cause an increase in sexual feelings.

☐ Oilier hair and skin can produce spots and pimples.

☐ There is usually a marked increase in sweating and body odour.

Changes at puberty (continued)

Changes that happen to boys

☐ The penis and testicles get bigger.

☐ The scrotum hangs lower and becomes looser.

☐ Hair grows on genitals, face, armpits and body.

☐ Sperm begin to be produced.

☐ The voice becomes deeper.

☐ The shoulders become broader and the body more muscular.

Changes that happen to girls:

☐ Breasts and nipples grow bigger.

☐ Ova (eggs) are produced and periods begin.

☐ Hair grows on genitals, armpits and body.

☐ The waist becomes more marked.

☐ The hips and thighs get rounder.

Young people need to understand what is happening to them and to their contemporaries of the opposite sex.

What concerns young people about sex

In areas of sex education such as these, there may be an advantage in using single-sex teaching groups.

Young men	Young women
Facial hair and shaving	Menstruation
Size and shape of penis	Size and shape of breasts
Scrotum, testicles and penis	Clitoris, vulva and vagina
Wet dreams	Buying and wearing bras
Voice changes	Buying and wearing tampons and towels
Spontaneous erections and ejaculation	Having a baby
Self-examination: testicles	Self-examination: breasts

Both Sexes

Body changes

Body image

Clothes

Spots and pimples

Growth spurts and clumsiness

Body hair

Body odour

Personal hygiene

Sexual organs

Being 'normal'

Orgasm

Masturbation

Gender roles and expectations

Sexual feelings

Appropriate behaviour

Romance, love and crushes

Being asked out and asking out

Being part of a group

Relationships with the opposite sex, friends and parents

Being allowed out

The ideal partner

Sexuality

Sexual intercourse

Virginity

Keeping safe

Contraception

HIV/AIDS

Sexually transmitted diseases

Everything about the opposite sex

'... provide knowledge about loving relationships, the nature of sexuality, the processes of human reproduction.' Circular 5/94.

How parents can help teenagers

Parents can provide stability and consistency for the changing adolescent.

☐ Create an open, supportive atmosphere at home.

☐ Take time to listen and talk, giving them your full attention. Try to pick a time when you are feeling good about each other.

☐ Accept that your son or daughter may have different views from you, but be firm on what is acceptable in your home.

☐ Negotiate rules and limits and adjust these as they get older.

☐ Be honest and straightforward; if at all possible, all adults in the household should present the same messages and a consistent approach.

☐ Respect their need for privacy.

☐ Young people sometimes say that they 'know all about it' in order to save embarrassment, yours and theirs. Don't take this at face value.

☐ Most parents do feel awkward talking to their children about sex. Be clear about what you value and how you feel about sexuality and relationships before you begin.

Sex Education, ages 11–18: a quick guide

- Remember that young people often want to talk about their feelings about sexuality rather than the 'facts'.

- Do not be too concerned if they prefer to talk to other adults rather than you. It can be hard for them to imagine their parents as sexual beings.

- Adults who go 'quiet' or ignore the mention of sex are giving the message that sex is secret and a forbidden subject.

- Remember that you cannot live your life through your child, that they need to learn by their own experience and that life has changed since your own teenage years.

- Remember that most young people do a lot more talking about sex and relationships than putting it into practice.

- Build up a sense of trust and treat them as responsible.

- This child/adult will keep changing his or her needs and roles, as if to confuse you. You, on the other hand, need to be the consistent adult for them, be tolerant of their mistakes, maintain a sense of humour and tell them that you love them.

'... parents are key figures in helping their children to cope with the emotional and physical aspects of growing up.'
Circular 5/94.

*The overall
intention of the law
is to protect young
people from abuse.*

☐ Under English law young people can marry at 16, with their parent's consent. They cannot marry without consent until they are 18. Under Scots law, young people can marry at 16 without consent.

☐ At 16, a young woman can legally enter into a sexual relationship with a member of the opposite sex. There is no such heterosexual 'age of consent' for young men.

☐ Over-16s are entitled to advice on birth control, abortion or any medical treatment without anyone's consent, provided the doctor or health professional believes that they are capable of understanding the implications of the treatment.

☐ A doctor or other health professional is not legally bound to tell anyone if he or she prescribes contraceptives or agrees to an abortion for a young person under 16; but guidelines from the Department of Health and Social Security encourage them to persuade the young person to tell their parent or guardian. According to these guidelines, the doctor or health professional should not normally give contraceptive advice or treatment without the parents' consent.

It is illegal for a man to have sex with a girl under 16, even with her consent. This applies to any male aged 10 or over. The law presumes that it is not possible for a boy under 10 to have sexual intercourse.

Women can only be charged with indecent assault on a boy under 16, not with unlawful sexual intercourse.

Young men cannot legally have a physical homosexual relationship under the age of 18. Even then, it is only legal between consenting adults in private, providing they are not in the armed forces. There is no 'age of consent' for female same-sex relationships.

The consent of a person under 16 cannot in law prevent an act from being an indecent assault.

It is against the law for a woman 16 or over to allow a man she knows to be her grandfather, father, brother or son to have sexual intercourse with her.

The Department of the Environment has advised that Section 28 of the Local Government Act 1988, forbidding the promotion of homosexuality, does not apply to sex education. Section 18 of the Education Act (No. 2) 1986 gives school governors responsibility for decisions on sex education in schools.

'Schools' programmes of sex education should aim therefore to present facts... and an awareness of the law on sexual behaviour.'
Circular 5/94.

The more the parents know about sex education, the more they can help their child with growing up.

☐ Look for books on sexuality, relationships and adolescence which you can read in order to understand and help your son or daughter.

☐ Look out for sex education resources at your local health promotion resources base or at the teachers' professional centre (leaving books or leaflets casually lying around to be picked up can be quite effective).

☐ Create an open, caring atmosphere at home in which your son or daughter can feel free to approach you with any concerns or questions.

☐ Take advantage of opportunities when they arise to talk about sexuality, listening to your son or daughter's comments with respect.

☐ Make sure that your son or daughter is aware of what is happening to their changing body, and that they know that everyone develops at different times and that different body shapes and sizes are normal.

IF YOU... want to share your child's sex education with the school

☐ Find out as much as possible about their school's sex education programme by:
- attending parent's meetings
- discussion with the school's Health Education Co-ordinator
- reading the sex education policy and curriculum statements

☐ Decide:
- whether you want to discuss certain aspects of sexuality before, at the same time as, or after the school programme, and how you will do it.
- what other aspects of sex education you want to discuss at home.
- whether there are aspects you want to leave to the school to teach.

☐ Take part in the development and review of the school's sex education policy and curriculum.

☐ Put your name forward to be a school governor.

☐ Ensure that you and the school are not giving conflicting messages; if there are different attitudes to some matters, discuss these with your son or daughter.

'What is learned at school can be supported by appropriate experiences at home and in the community.'
Curriculum Guidance 5.

IF YOU... want your child to be taught exclusively at home

'Where a parent wishes to discuss with the school possible ways of providing sex education at home, the Secretary of State hopes that schools will be ready to offer appropriate support.' Circular 5/94.

☐ Be sure of your reasons for withdrawing your son or daughter from school sex education and think carefully about the effect this may have on them.

☐ Be aware that they will most probably receive second-hand information from friends outside the classroom.

☐ Remember that you cannot withdraw them from National Curriculum aspects of sex education.

☐ If you do not want them to be taught at all, remember that ignorance or misinformation can expose them to embarrassment, distress and possible exploitation.

☐ If you want to teach them yourself, you need to feel sure that your own values, attitudes, knowledge and skills equip you to do so.

☐ Ask the school for help in finding appropriate resources for teaching at home.

☐ Decide on what you want to teach and how you will go about it.

IF YOU... are worried about your child's sex education

☐ Clarify what your concerns are and why you are worried.

☐ Talk this over with other adults whose opinions you respect.

☐ Look out for books on sexuality and relationships that you can read (see resource list at end).

☐ Find out about as much as you can about your son or daughter's sex education at school by:
  • attending parents' meetings
  • discussion with the school's health education co-ordinator
  • discussion with the head teacher
  • reading the sex education policy and curriculum statements

☐ Talk to a governor, preferably a parent governor or one who is closely involved with health education at the school.

☐ If you are still concerned, there should be a Health Education Adviser in your LEA who will be able to help you.

'Possible means of bringing all parents into the process include placing the topic in the annual report and on the agenda of the annual governors' meeting for parents, or holding specific meetings.'
Circular 5/94.

'In order to secure maximum support for their programmes of sex education, schools should ensure that both current and prospective parents are fully informed.' Circular 5/94.

- ☐ Has the school an up to date sex education policy?
- ☐ Is sex education carefully planned and co-ordinated?
- ☐ Does the school make sure it knows parents' views and wishes, and are parents encouraged to share in the planning and review of sex education?
- ☐ Do the school governors review the policy regularly?
- ☐ Have the staff received any training in teaching personal, social and health education, including sex education?
- ☐ Are the teaching resources up to date and relevant?
- ☐ Has the school library appropriate books on sexuality and relationships?
- ☐ Where and how is sex education taught?
- ☐ What is covered in the programme?
- ☐ Is there support from the head teacher and governors?
- ☐ Are other professionals involved? If so, who are they and how are they involved?
- ☐ Is the programme developmental, meeting the needs and maturity of different pupils?
- ☐ How does the school evaluate how effective the programme is?
- ☐ Are the needs and abilities of the pupils with special needs provided for?
- ☐ Is my son or daughter finding the programme useful and interesting and developing a positive attitude towards sexuality and relationships?

Key points about adolescence

Approval and appreciation from peers is very important.

Dramatic changes occur to the body at puberty.

Only they feel they are different: as their sexual identity develops, they may ask 'Am I normal?'

Lack of communication with parents may become a problem as teenagers become more independent.

Emotions are changeable and intense because of hormonal changes; teenagers can be very moody.

Size will influence expectations. People can expect more mature-looking teenagers to act like adults.

Clumsiness can accompany growth spurts and may produce feelings of inadequacy.

Educational changes are also taking place, such as new schools, decisions about subjects and careers, and examinations.

New outlook and approach to other people: intrigues, romance and crushes begin.

Cliques or social groups can emerge with their own culture in music, fashion, hairstyles, language and activities.

Enjoyment of this difficult time will depend on family support and love, self-esteem and positive relationships.

'... preparing them for the challenges and responsibilities which sexual maturity brings.' **Circular 5/94.**

Useful addresses

Brook Advisory Centre
153a East Street
London SE17 2SD
telephone 0171-708 1234

British Pregnancy Advice Service (BPAS)
Phone head office in office hours for
details of your local branch:
Unsty Manor
Wootton Wawen
Solihull
West Midlands B95 6BX
telephone 01564 793225

Childline
Freepost 1111
London N1 0BR
telephone 0800 1111

Department for Education
Sanctuary Buildings
Great Smith Street
London SWIP 3BT
telephone 0171-925 5555

Family Planning Association
27–35 Mortimer Street
London WIN 7RJ
telephone 0171-636 7866

Health Education Authority
Hamilton House
Mabledon Place
London WCIH 9TX
telephone 0171-383 3833

Health Education Board for Scotland
Canaan Lane
Edinburgh EH10 4SG
telephone 0131-447 8044

Health Promotion Agency for
Northern Ireland
18 Ormeau Avenue
Belfast BT2 8HS
telephone 01232 311611

Health Promotion Authority for Wales
Ffynnon-las
Ty Glas Avenue
Llanishen
Cardiff CF4 5DZ
telephone 01222 752222

Parentline
Westbury House
57 Hart Road
Thundersley, Essex SS7 3PD
telephone 01268 757077

Relate
Herbert Gray College
Little Church Street
Rugby CV21 3AP
telephone 01788 573241

School Curriculum and Assessment
Authority (successor to the National
Curriculum Council)
Newcombe House
45 Notting Hill Gate
London W11 3JB
telephone 0171-229 1234

Sex Education Forum
8 Wakley Street
London EC1V 7QE
telephone 0171-843 6000

Your local Health Promotion Unit or
Service is part of your Health
Authority and will be found in the
phone book under Health,
Department of, or local NHS trust.

Your local education authority (LEA)
will have an adviser or advisory
teacher who deals with sex education.
They can be contacted care of your
LEA (usually the county council or, in
cities, the borough council).

Sex education resources

Circular 5/94: The Education Act 1993, Sex Education in Schools, Department for Education.

Curriculum Guidance 5: Health Education, National Curriculum Council 1990.

Curriculum Guidance 8: Education for Citizenship, National Curriculum Council 1990.

Scilla Alvarado and Paula Paver, *The Inside Story: menstruation education for young men and women ages 9–16,* LDA 1993.

Hilary Dixon, *Chance to Choose: sexuality and relationships education for people with learning difficulties; an educator's resource book,* LDA 1991.

Hilary Dixon, *Yes, AIDS again: a handbook for teachers,* LDA 1993.

Hilary Dixon and Gill Mullinar, editors, *Taught Not Caught: strategies for sex education,* LDA 1989.

Gill Gray and Heather Hyde, *A Picture of Health: strategies for health education,* LDA 1992.

For young people:

Condoms, Pills and Other Useful Things, AVERT 1994.

Nick Fisher, *Boys about Boys: the facts, fears and fantasies,* Pan 1993.

Nick Fisher, *Living with a Willy,* Piper 1994.

Susan Meredith, *Growing Up: adolescence, body changes and sex,* Facts of Life Series, Usbourne 1985.

Gill Mullinar, *Sex Education Dictionary: a unique reference book for 12 years and over,* LDA 1992.

Alexandra and Iain Parsons, *Making it from 12–20: how to survive your teens,* Piatkus 1991.

Eleanor Stephens and J Bairstow, *Love Talk: a young person's guide to sex, love and life stuff,* Virago 1991.

Carol Weston, *Girltalk,* Pan 1993.

For parents and young people:

Answering Your Child's Questions, Growing up Series, Family Planning Association, 1991.

How Your Body Changes, Growing up Series, Family Planning Association, 1991.

Sexuality, Growing up Series, Family Planning Association, 1991.

Sheila Dainow, *How to Survive your Teenagers,* Sheldon Press 1991.

Elizabeth Fenwick and Richard Walker, *How Sex Works: a book of answers for teenagers and parents,* Dorling Kindersley 1994.

Nancy Kohner, *What Shall We Tell the Children?* BBC Books 1993.

Lynda Madaras, *What's Happening to my Body? a growing up guide for parents and daughters,* Penguin 1989.

Lynda Madaras, *What's Happening to My Body? a growing up guide for parents and sons,* Penguin 1989.

Condoms Across the Curriculum
Edited by Ian Harvey
ISBN 1 85467 180 4

Contraception
Pauline Maskell
ISBN 1 85467 218 5

Family Life Education
Dr Michael Kirby
ISBN 1 85467 210 X

HIV and AIDS Values
Alan R Gawith
ISBN 1 85467 230 4

How To Set Up A PSE Programme
Janice Slough
ISBN 1 85467 156 1

Personal Relationships
Dr Michael Kirby
ISBN 1 85467 178 2

Sex Education in Schools:
Study Materials A and B
Dr Michael Kirby
ISBN 1 85467 223 1 and 1 85467 224 X

Sexual Health, Assertiveness and HIV
Carol Painter
ISBN 1 85467 214 2

Support Materials for a Sex Education Programme
Dr Michael Kirby
ISBN 1 85467 229 0

Daniels Publishing resource packs are:

✓ *Fully photocopiable*

✓ *Ready for use*

✓ *Flexible*

✓ *Clearly designed*

✓ *Tried and tested*

✓ *Cost-effective*

Quick Guides are up to date, stimulating and readable A5 booklets, packed with essential information and key facts on important issues in education

Health education

Drugs Education for children aged 4–11: A Quick Guide
Janice Slough
ISBN 1 85467 310 6

Drugs Education for children aged 11–18: A Quick Guide
Janice Slough
ISBN 1 85467 311 4

Alcohol: A Quick Guide
Dr Gerald Beales
ISBN 1 85467 300 9

Smoking Issues: A Quick Guide
Paul Hooper
ISBN 1 85467 309 2

Sex Education: A Quick Guide for Teachers
Dr Michael Kirby
ISBN 1 85467 228 2

Sex Education for children aged 4–11: A Quick Guide for parents and carers
Janice Slough
ISBN 1 85467 312 2

Sex Education for children aged 11–18: A Quick Guide for parents and carers
Janice Slough
ISBN 1 85467 313 0

Career enhancement

Assertiveness: A Quick Guide
Chrissie Hawkes-Whitehead
ISBN 1 85467 305 X

Counselling: A Quick Guide
Chrissie Hawkes-Whitehead and Cherry Eales
ISBN 1 85467 302 5

Class and school management

Bullying: A Quick Guide
Dr Carrie Herbert
ISBN 1 85467 301 7

School Inspections: A Quick Guide
Malcolm Massey
ISBN 1 85467 308 4

Grief, Loss and Bereavement: A Quick Guide
Penny Casdagli & Francis Gobey
ISBN 1 85467 307 6

Safety on Educational Visits: A Quick Guide
Michael Evans
ISBN 1 85467 306 8

Equal Opportunities: A Quick Guide
Gwyneth Hughes & Wendy Smith
ISBN 1 85467 303 3

Working in Groups: A Quick Guide
Pauline Maskell
ISBN 1 85467 304 1

Organising Conferences and Events: A Quick Guide
David Napier
ISBN 1 85467 314 9

Working with Parents: A Quick Guide
Dr Michael Kirby
ISBN 1 85467 315 7

For further information

For further details of any of our publications mentioned in this Quick Guide, please fill in and post this form (or a photocopy) to:

Daniels Publishing
38 Cambridge Place   Tel: 01223 467144
Cambridge CB2 1NS   Fax: 01223 467145

Name ....

Job Title ....

Organisation ....

Address ....

....

Postcode ....

Tel No. ....

Fax No. ....

☐ Please send me details of the following publications:

☐ Please keep me informed of forthcoming Quick Guides and other
    Health Education Resources from Daniels Publishing

Have you ordered from us before? ☐ No ☐ Yes: account no..........

Notes

Sex Education, ages 11–18: a quick guide